Wilt

Stacey L. Pierson

ANUCI PRESS

This is a work of fiction. Names, characters, places, and incidents either are the product of the author's imagination or are used fictitiously. Any resemblance to actual persons, living or dead, events, or locales is entirely coincidental.

Copyright © 2025 by Stacey L. Pierson

All rights reserved. No part of this book may be reproduced or used in any manner without written permission of the copyright owner except for the use of quotations in a book review. For more information, address:

Tanuci69@gmail.com

First paperback edition 2026

Anuci Press edition 2026

www.anuci-press.com

Cover Design by Adrian Medina

http://fabledbeastdesign.myportfolio.com/

Edited by Robert Ottone

ISBN 979-8-9989778-8-6 (paperback)

ISBN 979-8-9989778-9-3 (eBook)

WILT

BY STACEY L. PIERSON

"For, before the harvest, when the blossom is gone and the flower becomes a ripening grape, he will cut off the shoots with pruning knives and cut down and take away the spreading branches."

Isaiah 18:5

CHAPTER ONE

PLANTING SEASON

There are two things Miles knew about himself: he had a garden of girls and he was fucked up.

Mist hovered over the lake as waves shook the rowboat. His scratched and busted knuckles grip the oars and row with ease. On the edges of a jean jacket, spots of blood have already soaked in. As he rowed, a smile appeared on his face.

Miles gazed at the water; aware he would be the one who broke the awkward silence.

"You make my life worth living. Adoring you is what makes me wake every morning," Miles said.

He guided the rowboat to the middle of the lake. A rusted anchor sat on its side, and with one hand, Miles picked it up and tossed it over. It hit the water with a hard splash. He watched it as it sunk into the dark shadows. He took a deep breath in the morning air. They were the only ones out this morning, and he knew it because the city truly didn't start until nightfall.

He peered over his shoulder.

"You're one of the most interesting and intelligent women in town. Anyone would be lucky to have you look their way," Miles said. "But you saw me."

He sat down and placed his arms on the oars, which were partially pulled up. The wooden grips dug into Miles' hands as they caused some pain, yet it excited him. Pain always woke a part of him that he had kept hidden deep inside. It was dark. Loud. And cold.

"I had it all planned out. I bought you the ring you wanted. I ordered your favorite flowers, which are now in the back of the store. I even asked for your hand in marriage from your father. And we both know how much he hates me," Miles said.

"I gave you everything," Miles said, he struck himself in the chest with each word. "And every piece of me."

He stopped. Despite the pain he inflicted on himself, deep inside the pain was sharp, and sickening as the word "betrayal" flashed like a neon sign with bulbs going out.

"And you just threw it all away. For him," Miles said.

The scene was breathtaking as they sat in silence. Early mornings were always over casted. The lake's surface was like dark glass as it rippled, broken against the sides of the rowboat. The dock they left from was a faded sketch in the mist.

"Don't you take any responsibility for the demise of our relationship?" Miles asked.

She ignored him. Miles grinned. He hated to be ignored. In one swift move, he lunged.

"Say something," Miles yelled.

Miles came face-to-face with the outline of a head that was wrapped in a black trash bag. He felt the garbage bag crumpled in his hand as he placed them. Silently, he counted to five and then exhaled. He broke the garbage bag with his fingers to reveal what was left.

With dried blood on her matted hair, it was hard to tell what color it was. Dark red lines which streamed out from the gash that reached from the back of her head to the forehead now were stained, along with dark black bruises were already formed under her eyes, and the left was closed, made it seem as though she were winking.

"Why couldn't you have loved me like I loved you?" Miles asked.

Chains crisscrossed from her chest to her waist and spiraled like a candy cane down each leg and finished to two large cinder blocks. He screamed at the top of his lungs. It bounced off the water as a small group of blackbirds and ducks scrambled away. He became angrier with every breath he took. The anger caused a shiver down his spine.

"Looking at you like this makes me happy," Miles said.

He took one last whiff of the strawberry and cream body lotion he put on her. His favorite. He pulled back. The wind had picked up, a strand of her hair covered her face, and Miles curled his fingers within it.

"How can something be so perfect, yet ugly at the same time?" Miles said.

He bent her head down and kissed right between the eyes. Feet on either side of the rowboat, Miles stood, then with all his strength picked up the woman's body.

"Don't worry, I'll come see you," Miles said. He put his lips only centimeters away from her ear. "I love you."

He dropped her.

The woman's body splashed into the water. She bobbed for a few seconds before Miles picked up the cinder blocks and tossed them overboard one by one. He glanced over the rowboat's side. He caught one last glimpse of her hair as she succumbed to the water's darkness. Miles knew then, she bloomed and became another flower in his garden.

The lake's surface was still.

Miles caressed the water. The water covered his fingertips. One final taste of her wouldn't hurt. He licked his fingers. His admiration for her has a frightening quality to it. He loved the way she fought him, the scratches on the back of his neck proved it. She was the best thing that ever happened to him. They all were.

Break-ups are difficult.

CHAPTER TWO

BEIGNET FOR YOUR THOUGHTS

1 1/2 YEARS LATER

Morning was always the same for Miles. And they started at LaSip, his favorite coffee shop, which was just two blocks from his job. He eyes the online pickup counter at the far end of the shop. He pushed his way through the crowd toward it while on the phone.

"What do you mean you are going to extend your stay?" Miles asked.

Almost to the counter, Miles listened to the person on the other line.

"No, no, no, I understand," Miles said after he made it to the counter. "I don't blame you. I just miss you. That's all."

Miles searched for his order in the sea of beignets, and coffee. He couldn't find them. Maybe he missed them. In the distance, he heard his name called. Head raised, he finally saw one of the employees staring at him from kitchen's side door. He motioned for Miles to come to him. And again, Miles made his way into the crowd, which had grown within the last few minutes.

"I know, I know. Like I said before you left. I'm not dating anyone and won't. Are you?" Miles asked.

On the other line was his girlfriend of six months, Elana Givens. She was a traveling nurse in California due to a nursing shortage at one of the county hospitals. It was hard for Miles. He wanted her there with him. But no matter what, he would make it work. He loved Elana.

Miles made it to the end of the employee door.

"I love you too," Miles said.

He got off the phone as the employee handed him a brown paper bag, and coffee.

"Here you go, Miles. Fresh out of the oven," a man said.

Miles snapped back into reality. In front of him, the man behind a counter stood with a toothy grin. It was Jay. One of Miles favorite people and it wasn't because he works at the best beignet bakery in town or because he always gave Miles a fresh batch, but because he cared about his job. Miles doesn't have to open the bag as the sweet, succulent smell of spongy beignets weighed heavily and warmed his hands.

"Thanks, Jay. You treat me right," Miles said.

"You're our best customer," Jay said.

Jay had sincere smile, one Miles never truly saw nowadays. To Miles, Jay was a myth, swamp legend – hell even a voodoo curse. And one Miles respected. As Miles began to pull out some cash, Jay stopped him. He did it only when he wanted something.

"Keep your money," Jay insisted.

"Are you sure?" Miles asked.

"Of course," Jay said as he waved the cash away. "Just make sure my sister has a little something special in her bouquet."

"I'll make it blend with her dress," Miles said.

"She'll love that," Jay said.

The place was getting packed. Miles dodged people in suits, moms in workout clothes, tourists who had never had a beignet, and even a chef from a competing restaurant down the road. Miles shock his head in amusement and never saw the woman's yoga bag strap on the ground until he got tangled in it. He tried to shake it and untie his ankle, when he lost his balance.

His drink splashed all over her.

The last of the coffee trickled out, the beignets destroyed after they were squished against a table when Miles tried to stop himself from falling. He stared. Her shirt was soaked.

"Holy shit," Miles said.

He watched as the woman gathered handfuls of napkins from a table nearby not caring who she disturbed.

"I am so sorry, I didn't see you," Miles said.

The first few words she said Miles didn't hear because her dark blue bra was more defined through the wet spots of the white shirt. Miles blinked and snapped back out of her stare when the woman snapped her fingers in his face.

"One thing I know is that you're not fucking blind. Didn't you see me? How hard is it to walk in a straight line?" the woman asked.

"A blind person walking in a straight line. I heard you," Miles said.

Unconvinced, the woman said, "Yeah."

She reached over the same table again. Her arm stretched between the couple as the woman pulled out more napkins. Miles was impressed by the way she didn't care they were there. She wiped down her white button-down shirt. She caught a glance at her watch.

"Fuck!" the woman said.

As she passed Miles, she slapped her napkin wad on his chest and walked past him.

"Thank for nothing asshole," the woman said.

He followed. He called out to her as she exited at the coffee shop.

"Look I'm sorry. I really didn't see you," Miles said.

"Ok, broken record," the woman said.

He liked her walk. It had an attitude. She wore an outfit not his favorite but seemed to fit her. Black leggings, semi-high boots, what looked like a faux black leather jacket, and no jewelry.

"How about I pay for your dry cleaning," Miles said.

The woman turned around, and walked backwards, "You wanna pay for this two-dollar shirt?" the woman asked.

"I do," Miles said.

"Fuck the shirt," the woman said. She held up a portion of her camera bag. "This is my life."

"What your name?" Miles asked.

"You first," the woman said.

"Miles," he said. "Miles Pike."

"I'll find you if I need you, *Miles*," the woman said.

He was in awe. She was unlike anyone he had ever met. And that made him grin. She was a bitch, but a cute one.

"It's Nora Asher," Nora hollered as she turned the corner and disappeared from Mile's view.

***

Many possibilities have rushed through Miles' mind as to who Nora was.

He walks down the semi-vacant sidewalk. The sun feels good, but it's going to be a hot one.

I can't lie, Nora, I can already see myself becoming obsessed with you. Were you the girl caught by the hated teacher in school smoking in the girls' bathroom? And like the rebel I know you are, you stare at her, take one last puff, and the smoke drifts from your black lipstick before dumping it in the toilet.

Miles walked down the middle of the street toward his job. It was normal to do that in New Orleans. It was safer in a way. It was more open, although the sidewalks were busy with construction, as others were blocked off, for whatever reason that day. However, the one different thing was the numerous "SOLD" signs posted on the front doors. In the corner of the sign a stood, Heathcliff Morand, in a teal suit; his teeth were bright and white, and he gave a thumb-up. His hair resembled that of a Ken doll—plastic and hard.

Miles watched as a man walked out of a street bar and set down a medium-sized chalkboard with the drink of the day written on it. He noticed Miles and waved. In return, Miles did the same.

From the corner clock shop to the organic cookie shop, Miles was reminded of Cathie. They used to eat the free samples every Tuesday; now he and a small bar were the last ones on the long street.

The most cunning real estate mogul in New Orleans had become a household name over the last year, buying up property, and now he wants Miles's flower shop. Miles hated to think about it and pushed it from his mind when he saw someone on a stoop up ahead.

"Morning, Davis," Miles said.

"Oh, hey boss," Davis said.

"What are you doing here so early? The wedding isn't until two," Miles asked as he unlocked the padlock.

"I know. But Renee needed space," Davis said.

"Renee," Miles said.

"Yeah," Davis said.

"Wanna talk about it?" Miles asked.

"Yeah. No. Yeah. I don't know."

It doesn't bother me if Davis doesn't want to talk about it. It's always something stupid. Once, it was who was going to take out the trash on a rainy day. I know, I know—I laughed about it too. But for them, it's a serious discussion. I think my favorite is who is going to clean out the litter box. I would love to hear something interesting like where to hide the body or how long it is going to take to bury a body in a six-foot grave.

Eight hours. It takes eight hours.

Miles unlocked the door and decided to keep his mouth shut with his opinion. But it was difficult. Davis wasn't a bad guy, and Miles remembered why he liked him so much. When Miles accidentally snipped the tip of his finger off, Davis had been captivated by the blood designs on the tissues Miles had tossed into the trash can. He thought that Davis might be able to help him one day, if that day ever came.

"You know if you ever need a place to stay. There's the apartment upstairs. You would have to move the storage boxes. But it's yours," Miles said.

A geeky smile and glazed-over look appeared on Davis's face.

"Really? Thanks, Miles. Can I?" Davis asked.

"Be my guest," Miles said.

"Awesome. I'll go get some stuff if she hasn't already tossed in the garbage," Davis said.

Miles watched as Davis took off.

"Guess I'll open this morning," Miles said as he walked inside.

***

One thing Miles learned from his mom is how to garden. She had a magnificent one. Speak of the devil. Miles's mother, delicate in her own right, generous, and above all honest, walked from the back through the door. Her long, straight as a board hair hung around the vase of lilies she carried.

"Morning, Miles," Mom said.

Her smile was infectious. Miles couldn't help but return it just as big.

Miles watched as his mom placed the vase in front of the bay window and gazed at the bright blue sky as the sun's rays filtered through the *Petal Perfection* yellow stencils on the sign and hit her soft angelic face. The name of the store always made Miles smile.

"Morning, Mother," Miles said.

***

Miles watched as his mom dug her hand into the wet dark soil with her bare hands. Gracefully, she took out a bundle of dusty pink and white morning glories. They looked like mini horns. She packed them into the hole, and Miles saw her smile.

"One thing about planting a garden is patience. You can't throw them in and expect them to do all the work. You have to love them. Talk to

them. Spend time with them. After all, a flower is a living thing," Mom said.

"Like the flowers in Alice in Wonderland?" Miles asked.

She laughed, "Exactly."

***

Miles stared at the customers as they checked out the flowers. Miles thought, *there's something about flowers that makes them mysterious but completely eye-catching. One, the petals are delicate, a wrong move or rub could destroy them, and their beauty will wither away. Some thrive in the sun, while others prefer to be hidden in the shadows. Sucking in the darkness. Feeding in the cold. Like me.*

And there goes the phone. It's going to be a long day. Miles hoped Davis would be back sooner than later. How busy could it get?

"I don't want blue. I want violet," the lady said.

Kill me. Kill me now. The more she talks the more I am praying for something to strike her down. I welcome death.

"I'm sorry ma'am, but we only have blue right now," Miles said.

"When will you have violet? I *have* to have violet," the lady said.

The way she said "violet" bothered Miles. It was like she held her nose and repeated the word. And she whined like a child. God, would it be splendid if Miles just grabbed her by her poorly dyed hair and slammed her head on the counter until she bled. The thought made Miles smile.

"I'll check. But the delivery truck doesn't come until..." Miles said

"I'll wait," the lady said.

"You'll wait?" Davis asked.

Relief washed over Miles as he saw Davis walk out from the back. Miles knew he could handle the conversation with the woman better without slitting her throat. That would be bad for business.

"Til Friday?" Davis asked.

"Excuse me?" the lady asked.

"I heard you say you were going to stay until the truck comes. That's Friday. I mean you can stay here with me in the apartment, but I have to warn you. My girlfriend says I fart in my sleep. So…"

"You are disgusting," the lady says.

"That's what she says. But still lets me sleep in the same room. I mean not this time. She did kick me out," Davis said.

"I can see why," The lady said as she looked Davis up and down.

Without another word, Davis walked off. She leaned in close to the counter.

"Where did you find him? The back alley?" the lady asked.

"Oh, yeah. The quarter is full of them," Miles said. "All I did was pluck out the best looking one."

The look on her face. Confusion. Miles could see the wheels inside her head as they turned. It took a few minutes, but she got the sarcasm.

"I'll be back Friday. And you better have them," the lady said.

"Violet daisies. Check," Miles said.

He watched her leave. Miles dreaded her coming back. He would just send Davis to deliver them. Mom walked up to Miles.

"People can be so rude nowadays," Mom said.

"Thank goodness I hold back," Miles said.

"Sometimes it hard not to," Mom said. "Before I forget. You had a visitor before opening this morning. They left their card, and a note for you."

Miles took it from her. His face flushed. He wasn't happy.

"Oh my. My poor boy is about to…" Mom said.

"Davis. I'm going to the mini-mart around the corner for peppermints. Watch the store for me," Miles said.

"No problem, boss," Davis said as Miles dashed out.

***

As he walked, Miles' thoughts drifted to Nora. *Nora, I can't tell you how many Elvis impersonators I've seen marry in-love couples and drunken Mardi Gras revelers. Tons.*

Walking in the mini-mart, Miles hovered his fingers over the shelves of peppermints.

"I swear I have it. Just gimme a minute to find it," a woman said.

I know that voice. No. This isn't happening. It can't be who I think it is. Holy shit!

"Here let me take some things out," the woman said.

Miles watched from around one of the endcaps as the woman laid her things on the counter. Nora Asher. Miles's heart pounded so fast at the sight of her He took a minute to get it together, calm himself. Yet, what a coincidence that he had seen her twice in one day. *What are the odds?* Miles took a deep breath.

"Hi," Miles said as he plopped a bucket of peppermints on the counter.

Nora looked at him and said, "Hey there, Miles."

"Looking for something?" Miles asked.

"He's gonna pay," Nora said. She smiled at Miles. "Dry cleaning."

CHAPTER THREE

A WALK TO REMEMBER

Miles watched Nora's arms swing back and forth, her right lightly skimmed his left. Through the sun's rays, he could see there was no hair on her arms. Miles thought, *Were you a swimmer? Competing for a chance at gold in the Olympics. They are so lean and tight.*

"Thanks for the jerky," Nora said.

"I owed you," Miles said.

Nora took a bite. Miles smiled.

"Did you ever make it your meeting?" Miles asked.

"Wow. I can't believe you remembered," Nora said.

Miles could tell she was impressed. He took a guess that most men who dated her never remembered the little things. But he did. He urged her for an answer.

"And?" Miles said.

"Pushy. I like that. Well, I did make it and sold a few photos," Nora said.

"I'm very proud of you," Miles said. "Even covered in iced coffee, you managed to make it happen. Awesome."

"I never thought a complete stranger would be encouraging," Nora said. "Thanks, Miles."

Only if she knew. It was a huge moment in Miles' mind. He was already invested in whatever they were blossoming into. He better ask the question that burned just to be asked. Before he rethought it, he blurted it out.

"Are you married?" Miles asked,

Nora laughed. It was nervous, Miles heard the shaken undertone. He either blew it or embarrassed her.

"Hell, no," Nora said. She took a large bite of her jerky and with her mouth full, she continued to talk, "I don't believe in marriage."

"Seriously. You don't believe in it?" Miles asked.

I have to know why. Maybe you were standing up at the altar, got a call, or one of your friends handed you a note. He was too scared to come and tell you himself. A cop-out I say. He's a fool.

"It's just a piece of paper. Big whoop. People sign contracts all the time," Nora said.

"Contract. Marriage isn't just a contract. It's about unconditional love. Devotion. Waking up, rolling over, and watching them sleep every day. Knowing they were made for you. They were put here for you and only you," Miles said.

Nora said nothing and that made Miles nervous. He wanted her to speak her mind because if he guessed, he knew he would get it wrong.

"What's her name?" Nora asked.

Miles was caught. At least, he felt that way. A fish caught in a net. He was sure Nora would want nothing to do with him now.

"Elana. She's a traveling nurse," Miles said.

They stopped at Petal Perfection.

"You work here?" Nora asked.

"I own it."

"Impressive," Nora said.

There was an awkward silence between them. Miles watched as she took a couple steps backward. Away from him. He wanted her to stay.

"I gotta go. But I know where to come when I need some flowers. Discounted of course, " Nora said. "See you around, Miles Pike."

Why do I have a feeling we'll see each other soon? Real soon.

"Who was that?" Davis asked, walking out.

"Fellow flower lover."

Miles watched her hips sway and form a figure eight in her black hip-hugger jeans with every step she took down the street. She made him forget about Elana and their relationship.

"When were you gonna tell me that we are catering Heathcliff Morand's party?" Davis asked. "We can't do that."

"Davis it's an opportunity I can't pass up," Miles said.

They walked toward the store.

"But he's trying to shut us down," Davis said.

***

Louisiana is famous for the food. Food is the one thing that sets it apart from all the other states. Shrimp etouffee, jambalaya, king cakes, gumbo, bread pudding—the list goes on. Savory and sweet. When it came to parties, food was king, but at this party the host was the entertainment.

Miles stood amidst a sea of flowers in various colors. He watched as servers lined up, waiting for their instructions. A few days prior, Miles received a map of the area in the house where the party would be held, allowing him to arrange the flowers properly. Soon, the servers were passing through the large entrance, each carrying a variety of flowers in their hands.

Time ticked, and Miles was anxious to leave. He usually was not there for the start of any party. He wasn't invited, all he did was deliver the floral arrangements.

Women in tight party dresses walked in alone or with their partners as they picked up flutes of champagne. Small groups began to cluster together, chatting loudly. They shared and talked about the houses and condos they sold, along with how much commission they received, as servers walked slowly with trays of food and drink.

Miles had enough. The night had already tired him out. And he wanted to go before the host arrived. Unfortunately, he knew it was too late when the guests began to clap. Miles weaved through the crowd. He peered over shoulders and saw Heathcliff Morand as he walked in. Miles watched as Heathcliff shook hands, patted several men on the back, and hugged a few of the women, who were more than happy to be near him.

Heathcliff smiled and hushed the crowd.

"I want to thank you for coming out tonight. This is a celebration, not just for me, but for all of us who are making changes in our community. Who want to extend the life of our city. We don't want to exclude people. We want people to invest in their future, and us real estate agents have a chance to build relationships to make that happen," Heathcliff said.

Miles listened as the crowd agreed by cheering him on.

"Now let's party," Heathcliff said.

The crowd cheered again. Miles were almost to the door. He wanted to avoid Heathcliff as much as possible. All he had to do was pass thought a small gaggle of people and he was free.

"Excuse me," Miles said.

Right as one of the men moved, Miles came face-to-face with Heathcliff.

"Miles Pike. So glad you could make it," Heathcliff said. He leaned close to Miles. "Why don't we do somewhere to talk. In private."

***

In Heathcliff's office, Miles watched as he poured two glasses of Bourdon. It was hot sitting in the leather chair. Miles felt himself sweating in places he shouldn't. Then, he noticed a blown-up photo above the fireplace.

Simple. Clean. Black and white. Around her waist, a white sash hung loose, it left something to the imagination as her breasts' curves peeked through the jacket she wore. Around her neck was a solid black tie. Her head was cut off, but Miles knew who it was.

Nora.

Heathcliff handed Miles one of the glasses. He noticed Mile's stare and pointed to Nora's picture.

"Interesting, isn't it?" Heathcliff asked.

"Yes. It is," Miles said.

Heathcliff sat in the chair angled next to Miles with a good view of the fireplace and Nora's photo.

"She's a local artist in town. Personally, I never heard of her, but my wife told me about her after she saw some photos in a small tent in the

French Quarter. So, when she offered me that," Heathcliff pointed, "I had to have it. She calls it *Soaked*. I just don't get the wet spots."

Soaked. Miles loved the title. It's the perfect title representation of Miles and Nora's coffee shop collision. Miles lifted his glass and held it near his mouth.

"She?"

Heathcliff took a drink, and said while swallowing, "Nora Asher."

Miles watched as Heathcliff's eyes darted around Nora's body in the photo.

I can only imagine the thoughts running through his mind. The different positions he would put you in. Tying you up to his bedposts as he kisses down your body. Not going to happen, I won't let it. Glancing at his desk again. Three-point five seconds. That's all I need to swipe the letter opener, stab it in, and drive it down to the tip of his hard head.

"The name sounds familiar," Miles said.

"Really? I'm surprised you know something besides the colored of dandelions and daisies," Heathcliff said.

"Why did you hire me for your...whatever it is out there," Miles asked.

Heathcliff placed his glass on the table in front of them. He sat back, and said, "I like a man who wants to get to the point."

"And that would be?" Miles asked.

"I was thinking I would invest in your flower business," Heathcliff said.

"Invest?" Miles asked.

"Yes. Life is getting harder, and things are becoming more expensive. What I want to do is help you to get ahead. Put some money in the bank," Heathcliff said.

"You don't want to help me. You want to own me," Miles said.

"I'm buying up the property around your flower shop and eventually you *will* be next," Heathcliff said.

"My shop isn't for sale," Miles said.

"Everything and every*one* are for sale. It's just about hitting the right price," Heathcliff said.

Miles set the glass down, then pulled out the check he received for catering the party. He ripped it up. Heathcliff chuckled. Miles threw the pieces of the check into the air. He then walked toward the door.

"I'm glad we had this talk," Heathcliff said.

Miles opened the door but stopped when he heard Heathcliff's voice.

"I always get my way one way or another," Heathcliff said. "You will sell. I will own your little garden."

CHAPTER FOUR

SILENT CONFESSION TIME

Nora, this is my confession.

As he walked thought the square, Miles couldn't help but talk to Nora, even if she wasn't there.

Relationships are like flower stems. Two people cannot build a strong foundation without water and care. The more a person put into it, the greener and more vibrant the relationship became. The ingredients are trust, honesty, loyalty, respect, and forgiveness. However, it must be equal. If only one person does all the work, the flower created will wilt. If one desired something, they should go into it with their entire heart, mind, and soul.

He was surprised when Nora jumped out in front of him.

"Smile!" Nora said.

After the flash and through black spots in his vision, Miles saw her. His heart raced.

"I don't think you smiled," Nora said as she peeked over her camera.

Miles rubbed his eyes, and said, "I wasn't ready."

Miles watched as she walked over to a small compact printer. Her ponytail bounced against her broadish shoulders, and she was toned. When she moved, Miles saw the muscles under her shirt flex. She was special and not his type. She had confidence and was fearless, unlike Miles, who was just average.

There's something under the edge of her shirt. *I didn't know she had a tattoo. Why would I? Not like that's something a person brings up immediately when they meet someone, saying, "I have a pair of wings on my shoulder."* She bent down and watched as Miles's picture printed out.

"Please tell me you smile on a regular basis," Nora said.

"I do. Just not when someone jumps out at me," Miles said.

"Sorry. But you didn't hear me when I called your name. I took the next best option. Here," Nora said.

"It's not bad," Miles said.

"You gotta be kidding me. Totally cringe," Nora said.

Miles imagined her sitting in front of a full-length mirror in mid-morning. Her hair was in a messy bun with wild strands that sway in the breeze coming through an open window. An oversized white shirt with the buttons halfway undone - nice bra - long enough for her to cover upper thighs, and her legs bent while she snapped a picture of herself looking through the camera with her lips parting.

"So, this is where you work?" Miles said.

"When times get tough, I have to do what I have to do. Even if that means taking random strangers' pictures for themselves, family, Christmas cards, or for memories while on vacation." Nora said.

I'm not a stranger.

"Well, thank you for this. My non-smiling makes me look like I'm scared shitless– I'll display this proudly behind the counter at work," Miles said, holding the picture up.

"Good. You better."

Dominant. Forceful. I like it.

"My customers will love it. I'll make sure they know you're the one who took it," I said.

She snatched the photograph from Miles' grasp, crumbled it, and tossed it over her shoulder as if it were nothing. *She didn't even ask me. She did what she wanted to do.*

"You can do better than that," Nora said as she lifted her camera again. "Your collar is cocked."

Excuse me?

She walked up and stood inches away from Miles's face. He could smell the faint scent of her sweet apple body spray and the shimmer of sparkles down her neck. She folded the corner of Miles's collar. He flinched as she reached for his eye. She held his arm tight as she swiped his cheek.

"It's a lash. As the saying goes, make a wish. It might come true," Nora said.

It already has.

Miles smiled. Nora stepped back and snapped a picture.

"Much better. You look nice when you smile. You should do it more," Nora said.

A compliment. Think of something. Give her one back. I like your boots. I like your long, slender legs. I want them wrapped around me as we fall on a feather bed. Deep and passionate kissing. I nip at your neck before I slide my tongue down your stomach, suck your outie belly button and place my hand on your chest. You moan as I twist and twirl you into ecstasy. All. Night. Long.

"What do you think?" Nora asked.

I think we need to fuck.

"I think you're right. So, how much do I owe you?" Miles asked.

"Forget it. On the house. Maybe when you see it, you'll think of me," Nora smiled, and handed over the picture.

I already do.

"Well, thank you. And I will. At least let me buy you a cup of coffee," Miles said.

"Make it coffee and a slice of pecan pie and you have a deal." Nora said.

***

Nora dropped the fork onto the saucer and leaned back in the chair. The sun beamed down, , and the stretched-out eyeliner narrowed her eyes like a cat. Her black fingernails drummed the beat of the light jazz music which played in the background. She swayed back and forth as she felt the music throughout her body.

Every breath she took, Miles felt his heart as it pounded in sync. The curve of her breasts peaked through her shirt's missing top three buttons. Miles imagined she slid everything off the table, grabbed Nora by the shoulders, and tossed her on top. With both hands, he ripped her shirt open. Kissed her breasts. In front of everyone and they would cheer me on and chanted his name like her was the star of the show.

"Earth to Miles?" Nora asked.

She placed her hand on his cheek, looked at him, and said, *"Yoo-hoo?"*

That's a strange thing to say.

"Sorry," Miles said.

"Where'd you go?" Nora asked with a half-smile.

"I have a lot on my mind," Miles said.

Miles darted his eyes to how Nora's grip on her glass got tight. The veins in her hand poked out. He found it interesting because he affected her. Mile wanted what she was thinking about.

"Tell me something about you," Nora said as she sat back in her chair.

"There's nothing much. I own a flower shop. Simple as that," Miles said.

"I have a feeling there's nothing simple about you," Nora said.

Nail on the head. I'm not simple, Nora. I'm as complex as they come. I want to yell it from the rooftops when I'm with you.

"What do you do when you're not," she waved her hand in the air, "flowering?" Nora asked.

I kill and plant girls who break my rules.

"That's about it. Flowers are my life," Miles said.

She slightly curled the side of her mouth as she looked me up and down. As she drummed the tips of her nails on the side of the chair, she squinted her eyes. It could be the sun, but Miles doubted it. He could tell Nora analyzed every move Miles made..

"What about you?" Miles asked.

"I collect old cameras," Nora said.

"That's interesting," Miles said.

"Are you always this uncomfortable when you try to get to know someone?" Nora asked.

Is this our first cringy awkward date? Because I have never been on one like this before. I have been set up on a few blind dates – none of e which have worked out. Don't worry, Nora – I never did anything to them. It just didn't work out. Not everyone is meant to be.

Nora threw her feet on the table, which shook it. Mils saw her loose red laces skipped a few silver loops while stared at him.

"I'll ask an icebreaker question. You game?" Nora asked.

She likes games. I can get used to it.

"Shoot.," Miles said.

Ok, give it your best shot. I love a challenge.

"Are you named after anyone?" Nora asked.

"No. Are you from here?" Miles asked.

"Born and bred. Favorite sexual position?" Nora asked.

She went for it. And didn't give a damn about anyone, especially those around who might hear our conversation. Miles already could tell Nora loved to shock people. It gave her a thrill, which gave Miles one. Miles knew he had to keep her on her toes.

"I don't have one," Miles said.

Lying seems like the best way to respond, But I do have one, Nora. I would like to show you one day, all week, the rest of the month – hell let's just fuck for eternity.

"Bullshit. Everyone has one," Nora said as she leaned forward in the chair.

She didn't expect it. Good, I need to keep her on her toes as she does me. It makes everything so much more interesting. Not like it already is.

"You?" Miles asked.

Nora chuckled and said, "Any one of them where I get to be dominant."

In her own special way, she's flirting.

"Favorite flower?" Nora asked.

"That's a hard one," Miles said.

Abby, Daisy, Savannah, Tabitha, Danica, Torrance – I have so many. Oh, wait she's not asking…she's asking about -

"It's a toss-up between sunflower and the classic rose," Miles said.

"You gotta choose one." Nora said as she tilted her head and stared.

I can't I loved them all. I still do to some extent.

"Ok, sunflower," Miles said.

"I expected you to say rose," Nora said.

"My turn. How do you find your inspiration?" Miles asked.

"It's all around me. And in front of me," she said.

And you're in front of me.

"Bonus question," Miles said. "Don't you think it's weird we keep running into each other?"

She's going to ask about Elana. I better beat her to the punch.

Nora laughed, pulled her feet down, leaned forward, and said, "Guess it's fate."

I completely agree with you, Nora.

Glancing around, I see the time. 2:45.

"I have to go. I have customers and deliveries to make," Miles said.

Nora gathered her things and downed the rest of her iced coffee.

"I'm walking you to work," Nora said.

She tucked her hair behind her ear, and her hand dropped to her side. Miles wondered what she would do if he grabbed her hand, dragged her into the alley, and threw her up against the wall.

"I looked you up on social media. You have accounts, but you're not active. You're not even that active on Petal Perfection's page. But I see you all over your…girlfriend's page," Nora said.

So, she has been looking. She's more than interested in me. I can see her staring at her screen, furiously searching, looking for something, anything about me. Always coming back to Elana's page, staring at me.

I wonder what else she does when she thinks about me? I wonder how I make her feel.

"If you want more business, then you have to reach out," Nora said.

"I do well," Miles said.

I don't, but you already knew that didn't you Nora?

"But you could be doing so much better. I can help. Wait," Nora said as she stepped in front of Miles, "Call me. I could make you killer photos to bring more business."

Face to face, we looked at each other. She dug inside her bag, retrieved a pen, peeled back my fingers, and I felt as she wrote inside my hand. We knew we were in the way of the customers as they walked in and out of Petal Perfection, but I didn't care, and I'm sure she didn't either. We were the only ones who existed in that very moment.

"First one is my cell, and the second is my job," Nora said.

"I thought you were a photographer," Miles said, as he stared at bottom number. "The second number looks familiar."

"It's the New Orleans police department, district nine," Nora said.

Holy fuck!

"I guess I know who to call if there's a break-in or I'm in trouble," Miles said.

"I work in the lab. I'm a crime scene photographer. But if you *did* need something I know who to call," Nora said. "I'm a night owl, so call me anytime if you want."

I'm not sure if I should feel relieved or guarded.

Nora held Miles's hand for a little longer than he expected. He felt her touch caress the numerals directly above hers. Miles sensed she didn't want to leave, and he didn't want her to either. Miles's phone rang. Nora let go. Miles dinged with a text.

Nora smiled, and Miles noticed that while she dug her foot into the ground, she moved back and forth. Miles thought, *I bet her leg muscles are strong*.

"Better get to those deliveries," Nora said. She pointed to his pants pocket. "And don't forget to answer…Elana." She winked.

He watched for the second time as Nora walked away from him. He reached into his pocket and answered his phone.

"Hey, babe," Miles paused and listened. "No, it's not a bad time. I was helping a customer."

CHAPTER FIVE

MAKE SURE THEY'RE DELIVERED

Miles stood behind the counter, taking an order for flowers when a man approached. He placed a bouquet of white roses on the counter. Miles turned and smiled as he finished his phone call.

"I'll take these," the man said.

"Roses are always the best choice," Miles said.

"My girlfriend deserves them. She puts up with a lot," the man said.

"Do you want these in a box, or wrapped at the stem?" Miles asked.

"Wrapped and delivered. And..." The man bent down, grabbed a small bundle of wildflowers, and dropped them down on the counter like they meant nothing. "These too. Box them. Make them look expensive," the man said.

Miles spotted the tan line on his ring finger. Miles knew the wildflowers were for his wife, and the roses were for his lover. Water dripped from the wildflower stalks and onto the countertop. He took out a black American Express card and handed it to Miles.

Miles knew the man didn't want to buy them. He was doing what he had to do to prevent his wife from discovering the truth by not using his personal card. It wasn't the first time and wouldn't be the last. Miles took the AMEX card and turned to run it. He paused. It wasn't the name on the card that piqued his interest. It was where he worked. Morand Enterprise, as in Heathcliff Morand.

"Is there a problem?" the mas asked.

"No. Just spaced out for a minute," Miles said. "It's been a busy week."

After the card was run, Miles gave it back and motioned toward some blank cards.

"Oh, don't forget to fill out the card. I think a personalized note means so much when getting flowers," Miles added.

Miles wrapped the roses in white paper, tied them with a long brown string, and placed them inside a white box. With the wildflowers, he did as he was told. He placed them in a small box, and sealed them with a heart sticker. He hated that he enclosed such beauty, that were small but gorgeous, then his gaze shifted to the pair of shears he used to snip the brown string.

All I have to do is snip it off. While I'm at it, I need to snip off his toupee. Along with his ear. Or both. Maybe sending his wife blood flowers will make her happy. I know I will be.

"Make sure the roses get delivered today or I'll post a bad review," the man said.

Before he left, he knocked out a few wildflower bundles onto the floor.

"Have a nice day," Miles said.

Miles walked around the counter, bent down to pick them up when he was reminded of Abby. She was his first.

Abby had a charm and beauty that were undeniable. Miles loved the way her skin felt next to his. She used to walk her fingers up his arm while she made small circles every few steps as her black hair dangled over her rich dark brown eyes. She was breathtaking. She flirted with other guys, but that was her personality. Miles accepted it because she was with him, not them.

Then Miles learned the truth about her. She let the past come back to haunt her—them. It ruined everything. Rule one: never let the past come between them. She broke it. He did what he needed to do.

**

Miles sat higher on Abby's back as he listened to her gasp and watched as she tried to curl her fingers around his leather belt which was wrapped around her neck. Miles watched as one of her clear-coated fingernails broke off. He always loved her nails.

The harder she tried to pull to get free the more Miles tightened the belt wrapped around her neck. There were pieces of her black hair which snagged underneath it. It was so shiny, long, and beautiful. It was one of the reasons Miles fell for her.

Miles didn't expect her phone to ring.

Miles clenched his jaw as sweat rolled down the sides of my cheeks. He reared back and jerked hard.

Her neck snapped. Abby went limp. Miles dropped Abby's body with a thud.

"Abby, please tell me that you didn't make plans and forgot to tell me," Miles said.

***

The elevator was the worst one Miles had ever been on in New Orleans. Every single piece of the paneling was cracked and looked like it would fall apart any second. He looked up through the open ceiling and listened as the gears grinded against one another. It reminded me of Sadie.

She was something else. Despite the overdrinking and the occasional cigarette here and there, Miles was in love. And with support, Sadie quit and became a new person. The right person Miles wanted.

***

As Sadie struggled and fought to break free from the sewn-up sleeping bag and his tightened grip, Miles smiled and continued to drag it and her against the loose rocks, logs, and occasional dips.

"I have always loved your fighting spirit, Sadie. It was just one thing that attracted me to you, besides your low tops. I thought once we were together – you would have realized that you didn't need to wear that kind of stuff anymore. I mean you had me," Miles said.

"Let me outta here, Miles," Sadie yelled through the sleeping bag.

"I can't do that. See you forgot one thing about being in a relationship - ask permission before you share intimate details about our relationship with other people. Especially your piece of shit friends," Miles said.

Sadie screamed.

"Come on. Don't scream. How are we supposed to have a constructive conversation if you're screaming at the top of your lungs?" Miles asked.

Sadie kicked and screamed louder. Miles rolled his eyes and dropped her. As he stood above, he watched as Sadie tried to break the sewn zipper.

"I asked... how can we have a constructive conversation when you're screaming. See this is what I'm talking about."

He reared his foot back and kicked her several times. She grunted screamed out for help. Out of the corner of his eye, a long piece of wood lay nearby.

She always wanted to try bondage. How about some nature bondage? The log is thick, curvy, and weightless to Miles. But heavy when it came down on Sadie. Sadie slowed down as Miles bought it down repeatedly o her body and head. He listened as her moans of pain became more muffled. Then stopped.

He was happy for some quiet time.

"Well, it's about time you're seen and not heard," Miles said.

Miles picked up the sleeping bag. It' felt heavier than it was. He struggled for a moment before he got his balance. Once he did, Miles walked toward the dock.

"It's that old saying, 'think before you speak.' How hard was that? No one needed to know abut our relationship, especially our sex life," Miles said.

Miles dropped Sadie into the rowboat waiting at the lake's shore.

"Seriously, it wasn't that bad. I mean...I made you scream," Miles said as he stared down at the blood-stained sleeping bag.

Miles climbed in and the further they drifted away, the more they became part of the darkness.

***

Miles glanced down at the box of roses in his arms. He should have asked Nora what her favorite flowers were. Roses were too ordinary for Nora. Maybe a dead snapdragon would be more her style. Their petals are curved to form skulls, and their stems are black with gray thorns. He decided to order some since it would take a long time if he grew them. He stood outside apartment nineteen. He knocked. Through the door, he heard a woman's voice.

"Coming," a female voice called.

Miles waited for the woman to unlock the door as he heard the clicks of her shoes approach. As she flung open the door, sunlight from inside the room illuminated the side of Miles's face.

"I was wondering what took you so long. I've been waiting for you," the woman said.

The woman stood in the doorway in a short, lacy black piece of lingerie that ended just above her thighs. The plunged V-neck revealed her breasts as oval-shaped holes hugged her sides. She had red heels on. Now Miles knew why her steps sounded like stutters. Shocked, Miles's face turned flush. He felt the air in his chest get sucked out.

"Miles!" Elana exclaimed.

"You're supposed to be in California," Miles said.

"What are you doing here?" Elana asked.

"I just talked to you on the phone. How are you here?" Miles asked.

"I can explain," Elana said.

CHAPTER SIX

WHAT COULD HAVE BEEN

Miles leaned on the counter; Miles felt another vibration. Miles wondered, *how many texts can one person send?* Before he could respond to one, Elana was sent another, and another. He had come to the realization a long time ago that *nature* was who she was. Miles thumbed through the photo, a picture of her trail leader Matt, dozens of pictures of trees, and different colored leaves, bugs, and dark trails, but one was his favorite. Elana with a wildflower in her hands as she took a selfie. It was soft, Miles wished he was there with her.

Then he got a text that read, *Gotta go. Love you!* Not the most interesting conversation, but it would do. A winky face with its tongue out. Maybe they could work this out. Yes, he was shocked when she opened the door in the outfit, but Elana was worth it. And he knew it.

"Hey boss," Davis said.

"What is it, Davis?" Miles asked.

"He's on the phone again," Davis said as he twirled the receiver in a circle.

"Who?" Miles asked.

"Heathcliff Morand. He wants to talk about selling this place. You're not selling, are you?" David asked.

"I hope not," a familiar female voice sings across from the other side of the shop.

Miles snapped his head to the right to see Nora as she walked in. Shocked to see he, Miles's lips parted.

Nora! What a sight for sore and tired eyes.

The sun, along with Miles, followed Nora's every step as her hips swayed. To Miles, they sang his name; he glanced down to see her hands swing while her fingers curled into her palm. The clicks of her boot heels echoed all around Miles like the ringing of church bells as she made her way toward him. Suddenly, Miles realized that slow-motion was her friend and lover. He wanted to be her lover. He wanted to love. He knew right away he wasn't going to let her down. Not like I did, Tabitha.

Tabitha.

***

Her long blonde hair flowed down to the middle of her back. Tabitha stepped inside a dark Petal Perfection, with the exception of two flames, which flickered. Set on a small round table in the middle of the room, two white plates with grilled fish and veggies sat along with two champagne glasses ready to be filled with the mineral water. Tabitha didn't drink. She smiled as she set her light blue eyes on Miles.

"I thought after the week you had, you could use a break," Miles said as he gestured toward the chair he had pulled out for her.

"You thought right. But you didn't have to do all of this," she motioned as she walked over, and Tabitha said, "All of this. It's too much."

"Nothing is too much for you. I swear I haven't done enough since you have been working late on your presentation; I am so proud of you."

Between the Hawaiian sauce drizzles on the fish, and her perfume, Tabitha smelled like salty ocean breezes with sweet floral notes of hibiscus and plumeria.

"You remembered," Tabitha gushed. "I told you that story, what—two times? Color me impressed.

I opened the dark blue water bottle and began to fill her glass. He bent with the pour and whispered near her ear.

"I remembered everything you said you liked, loved, wanted, needed, and wished for... Let's dig in."

Miles took a bite, and Tabitha raked the edges of her fork over the fish as it mixed with the light-yellow sauce. Miles noticed.

"Something wrong? Is it overcooked, under?" Miles asked.

Tabitha dropped her fork, and said, "No. How about we skip dinner and go straight to dessert?"

Tabitha stood and leaned ns over the table, her hands on either side to maintain balance as she started to climb and pushed everything away. She's going to fall. Miles grabbed her as she reached around his neck and pulled him into a deep and hard kiss. Miles pulled back.

"What?" Miles asked.

"Nothing. I love it. But..." Tabitha said.

Tabitha sighed heavily and loudly. Miles could tell she was upset. She slid off her chair and walked to the middle of the room.

"I need more than a break from work, Miles. I have tried to make this work. I need more than this—I need someone who can keep up with me," Tabita said,

"I don't understand. You're breaking up with me?" Miles asked.

"No, no. I'm not. I want to bring in someone else. Well, for me. Not you, " Tabitha said.

Miles physically shook his head, while he tried to form words. No one had ever said this to him before.

"You don't get it," Tabitha said as she walked toward Miles.

"So, you want sex, not love," Miles asked, confused.

Tabitha walked then placed her hand on Miles's chest, He hoped she felt his heart as it pounded, and hoped it landed in her hands to have her breathe new life.

"Yeah, I do. With you, it gets a little boring, average, and simple, like a Hallmark movie, not porn," Tabitha said.

Her hands slid off his chest after two quick taps as Tabitha turned to walk away. Out of the corner of his eye, the flames danced off the blue water bottle. With narrowed eyes, Miles noticed Tabitha's hair move rapidly as she spoke. Nothing she said was anything Miles wanted to hear. He gripped the bottle, took it off the table, and held it at his side as he approached her.

"I don't share, Tabitha," Miles mumbled.

He hit her on the back of the head so hard, she stumbled forward and caught herself against the wall. Miles watched as she started to hyperventilate after she saw blood in her palms. Within seconds, Tabitha tried to open the door, but the blood on her hand caused her to slip from the doorknob.

Miles loved it when they were scared.

"I hear what you're saying. But here's the problem I am having, " Miles said.

Tabitha pulled herself to the door. But Miles watched as she lost her balance. He knew then she was in pain and confused. On her face, she winced and attempted to touch her head, Miles liked the pain she was in. He wanted to inflict more.

"Stand up," Miles said.

"What?" Tabitha asked, her voice trembling.

"I said, stand up. I know you're not that hurt. I want you to be as tough as you act with others. With me. So, stand up. Do you want me to help? My hands are calm," Miles asked.

Tabitha flinched when Miles stepped close.

"Take it and show me what you've got," Miles said, offering her the bottle. Miles screamed, "I said take it."

The second she took it, Tabitha swung. Miles knew that was going to happen. He knew her too well, better than she did herself. Miles kicked her in the stomach. She hit the wall next to the front door as the bottle slipped from her hands and made a thud.

"It's funny how no one ever looks where they are going in my shop." Miles stepped closer, and said, "As I was saying earlier, I have a problem with the whole thing. I don't share."

Miles shoved her with every word. When she couldn't stand, he picked her up. He spat in her face and threw her away from him. And then she stopped. With eyes wide, Tabitha's breathing slowed, her hand shook, and then her body went limp.

"Now look what you did," Miles said.

He had tossed her against the wall and caused a long nail to become embedded into the back of her head.

"You have gone and ruined our romantic dinner by falling against a few of the fern plant hooks. Well, at least you don't have to worry about stitches," Miles said.

He turned around, walked to the table, and sat down. He chugged whatever water was left in his glass. He didn't feel like water, that was Tabitha's thing. He went behind the counter and pulled out a bottle of red wine. As he sat down, he heard Tabitha's deep gurgles as life left her body. He was starving. Bite after bite, the noises Tabithia made, she interrupted his meal. He slammed his fist on the table and shouted.

"Do you mind hurrying up and dying? The sun is going to be up soon, and I prefer not to get caught," Miles said.

He poured another glass of wine and held his glass to her.

"Cheers," Miles said.

***

"Hi," Miles said.

There's no doubt about it. He felt heat in his cheeks as he reddened with slight embarrassment. Nora had this power over Miles that he couldn't explain, but he liked it.

"Please tell me you're not selling?" Nora asked.

I didn't know she was coming today.

"Uh, boss. What do you want me to do?" Davis asked as he held his hand over the phone.

"Just hang up on him, Davis. He's nothing more than a leech with money," Constance said.

"No. It's not for sale," Miles said as he never took my eyes off Nora.

"I am outta here. Don't call me Davis. I'm going for a drink," Constance called out as she walked away toward the back of the shop.

Davis shrugged and hung up. He couldn't stop looking at her. Nora glanced around; she smiled. Miles thought Nora's cheek dimples were the cutest. They weren't too deep or too small; they were perfect, just like her. She moved away and glided her fingertips across the blossoming orchards, which painted her hand blue, pink, and yellow. The vines of baby's breath tickled her ears, and she laughed as she bent down to smell the white roses in the stormy-colored vase.

Nora, which flower is your favorite? I'll give it to you. If I don't have it, I will get it. I'll get you whatever you demand.

"What can I help you with?" I ask.

"So *professional*," Nora says.

Miles licked his lips as Nora took off her sunglasses. He was the only audience member who sat in a red velvet chair, he gripped the arm of it as if someone had the spotlight on her. At the same time, she was the center of the stage as flower petals fell all around her.

"After having such an incredible talk, the other day about positions and flowers. I would think we would have something a little more intimate happening between us," Nora said.

Can I rip your clothes off or should I wait for closing time?

"Bad habit. I'm always in work mode," Miles said.

"Is that what you call it?" Nora asked.

Miles loved the smirk on her face. Her wink, combined with her infectious smile, made Miles grin ear-to-ear. She made the day bright and worth living.

"I have a proposition for you," Nora said.

Trying those different positions? Count me in. How about the counter? It's sturdy.

"Shoot," Miles said.

"A magazine has hired me to do a photo shoot and I have the chance to do whatever I want," Nora said.

And you thought about me.

"And you're thinking?" Miles asked.

"Flowers. Tons of flowers. I can see it in my head, but I need your help to make it come to life. And I need your flowers. I *want* your flowers," Nora said.

Flowers I have.

"Peonies, tulips, snapdragons, and pink roses are the favorite this year," Miles said.

Miles gestured toward the open flower to the dozens of flowers.

"What do you need? Bold, saturated colors like mustard yellow, or cobalt blue. Sustainable & Eco-Conscious florals with berries and herbs. Maybe a nostalgia vibe with delicate and soft colors plates with a vintage vase hence the name vintage revival. Or you could go with one of mom's favorites," Miles picked up a bundle of artisan farming flowers, "Dusty lavender mixed with some other seeds farmers cross breed to make amazing and unique combinations," Miles said.

Nora slipped her sunglass back on, and said, "That was a lot, and I'll take them. Be at my place on Tuesday at twelve."

Nora handed Miles a slip of paper with her address on it. Her handwriting was as curvy as her breasts, which Miles glimpsed through her black shirt. Miles figured she knew what she was doing because she was halfway unbuttoned. Miles saw the chain around her neck that dangled between them. With a half-smile, she slightly bobbed her head. She wanted him to look.

She's flirting with me.

"Which ones do you want?" Miles asked.

"Surprise me," Nora said.

She grazed against Miles's shoulder.

"I trust you," Nora said.

Miles knew she could have easily stepped to the side or twirled around him, but she didn't. It meant something. It meant something to Miles. He watched as she swayed her hips side to side more noticeably than before. As she stepped over the threshold out of the shop, Miles didn't want her to leave.

Don't let her leave. Think of something. I know.

"I was thinking about what you said about more exposure for the shop. I think you're right. I need help. If you're still up for it," Miles said.

She stopped and said, "I'm up for it. I'm up for anything."

Here's my chance.

"Maybe we can get together and talk about it tonight," Miles said.

"I can't. I have a date," Nora said.

Who's the lucky guy?

"Oh. Oo-kay. Um, I'll call you. Or you can just call me. Or come by..." Miles said.

Nora placed her hand against the doorframe. The way she drummed her fingers against the wood made Miles wish *he* was that doorframe right now.

"What's your favorite place to eat around here?" Nora asks.

She knows places around here. She's asking so I can know where she is. It's an invite to crash her date.

"Dolly's Diner is my favorite. They have the best burgers in town," Miles said.

"Too bad my date is vegan. But my body *does* need some meat," Nora said.

Miles watched as she left.

I accept your invitation.

CHAPTER SEVEN

ONE, TWO, THREE, AND MORE

Spoons hit the side of coffee cups as they were stirred, napkins were yanked out of the small silver dispensers, and people laughed and talked all around Miles as he sat at the diner.

The last time Miles was there was with Elana. He listened to her talk about the trails and how she wanted to make a change in how people viewed hiking. Miles watched as Elana pulled out her phone and reposted articles on hiking and how to survive when one is lost. But Nora. She's different. She's open to some change and not afraid of her hands getting sticky from the menus. Miles's thought, *where is she? And why am I so nervous.* He checked his watch. He should have asked Nora when she was coming. Or at least get some sort of idea. It felt like forever since he sat in the booth.

"You have been here forever," a female voice said.

Miles looked up and saw his mom across from him with overlapped hands as she stared with her bright eyes and warm smile.

"Mom? What are you doing here?" Miles asked.

Miles's left hand begun to tremble.

"What? You want me to leave?" mom asked.

"Well, yeah, I do. I don't think I want Nora to meet my mother this way," Miles said as he leaned close.

"But I wore my favorite outfit," mom said.

She held out her hands and referenced the white sundress with little yellow roses that danced around as ringlets of her long black sliver tone hues sprinkled through the strands, with her simple gold wedding band.

"I want to meet her. From the way you stare and talk about her. I just assume she's the next bright light in your life. Besides *me* of course," Mom said.

The tap on the booth's table seemed so real. Miles watched as she noticed the fake flower in the peeling paper vase. She chuckled as she picked it up. Eight years ago, Miles's life changed. He knew what he did but never took on full responsibility. He did what he had too.

"You would think they would use real flowers by now. I mean the ambiance is missing. Real is the most important thing nowadays. Don't you think?" mom asked.

With every peel of the paper flower, Miles felt like he had been peeled back. His heart raced, his breathing caught in the middle of his throat, he had to shift his jacket from his sweating skin for it to breath, and he felt thousands of invisible pine needles prick his arms.

"Mom. You're not real," Miles said.

The tremble in his left hand was getting out of control. Miles slipped his hand under the table.

"I'm as real as you make me," mom laughed.

Her laugh was strong and whimsical, like the wind blowing through the windchimes she and Miles made when Miles was seven. He made sure he buried her near it so he could always remember her when it chimed.

"Can I give you a little advice?" mom asked.

"I'm all ears," Miles said.

"That makes one of us, doesn't it?" mom remarked.

She's still making jokes after that night. Good for her. I'm glad she seems happy. Happier than before at least.

She placed the stem of the fake flower behind her ear. It tilted but her hair held it. Miles remembered that day like it was yesterday.

"Women are delicate. Gentle. Not like Elana. She is a piece of work. But Nora, I love her. I love her for you. She gives you a run for your money. You need that. I need that," mom said.

"You do?" Miles asked.

"Oh, yeah. She's the total package. She has substance, and a lot of spunk. She knows what she wants and how to get it. She comes from strong roots, and she will never falter under pressure through the rain, heat, and even a hurricane," mom said.

"She is something. Isn't she?" Miles asked.

"*Something* isn't the word," mom said.

"I think I found the one," Miles said.

She reached out and touched his cheek.

"My little boy. My heart. My flower. I am so happy for you. You are going to be as happy as your dad and I were," mom said.

And like that the pit in Miles's stomach dropped like going down a roller coaster's dip fast and hard. Like her and his dad. He became nauseated at the thought, and the impending doom he felt overcame him.

***

His mother waited for Miles at the bottom of the stairs as he approached. She was going through her purse and kept checking the time. But Miles was too scared to go down. His father was angry and never took his dark narrow eyes off her as he spoke slowly and steady, His words sounded like a growl.

"What's keeping him? You need to go up there and drag him down the stairs. If I am late, I am going to remind him why we can't " dad said.

"I know and we won't be. How about you go, and we will meet you there? I will come up with something, " mom said.

Miles hated being home. Most of all he hated his father.

Mom stepped away but dad grabbed her close and looked down at her.

"I can see the extra weight in your ass and stomach. Most women care about what they look like. But you don't," dad said.

Miles never understood why dad was so mean to mom. To Miles, she was the best. He hated him when he was. After his dad left, Miles headed downstairs and wrapped his arms around her tire. He loved her just the way she was. She was perfect.

Dad popped her on her butt and left out the front door. Miles rushed down the steps and to his mom. He wrapped his arms around her waist and buried his face in her chest.

"I hate him, mother," Miles said.

"I do too. But no worries," mom said low to herself.

She forced a smile on and bent down to Miles. She dug inside her purse and retrieved a small yellow rose pin. She pinned it onto Miles's collar.

"Now this makes you more handsome than you already are, baby boy," mom said.

"I'm never going to take it off," Miles said He looked at it in an angle. *"What happens when it wilts?"*

"Don't be silly, pins don't wilt. But if a flower does, then place it in water, and bring it back to life. It's going to be hard, But I have faith you can – will do it," Mom said.

***

Miles felt the coldness from her touch, but still, her hand was soft. Underneath her long natural fingernails, mud sat, hard and dried. Her smell was wet. Miles closed his eyes and leaned into her hand.

"You're nothing like your father. But you have to go by the rules I taught you. It's the only way to be truly happy. And have the sun warm your growing garden. Why don't you tell me what you want?" mom asked.

"Excuse me? Hello?" a female voice asked, rough as if she had just smoked a carton of cigarettes.

Miles opened his eyes. His mom was gone. There was a sadness that crept inside his heart. I really missed and loved her.

"I haven't got all night," the waitress said.

She hovered over Miles, and by the looks of her she had been there for a long time. When he looked up at her he noticed she had bags under her eyes and smacked her gum like she was still hot shit, which she was not.

"Sorry," Miles said.

"Wanna tell me what you want?" the server asked.

"Uh, water," Miles said.

"Water?" server stood there with a dumbfounded look. "Is that all?"

"Yep. Just water," Miles said.

She rolled her eyes and walked off. Miles became nervous. He thought, what am I doing? I shouldn't be here. Nora might think this is too consequential.

Miles heard her laugh. Nora walked in with her date. Miles could see her arm entangled within his. Miles focuses on her bracelets as she tightened her grip. He watched as they walked over to an empty booth. He didn't want her to see him. Miles sunk down some in his seat, so he wouldn't be seen. He glanced every now and then at them, it was a miracle for Miles when Nora's date is headed for the bathroom, and she is putting her head on the table. Perfect.

The server set Miles's water down as he hopped up and pretended like he was on the phone. Fate had other plans and Miles was about to find out as the busboy is on the other side of the aisle turned. Miles and the busboy, who had just finished clearing a table, collided. The sound was loud and might as well have been a stake jammed into Miles's heart because everyone stared. Nora popped her head up.

So much for sneaking out.

Miles and the busboy were surrounded by plates, silverware, and food. Miles helped him up as half-eaten tomatoes along with what looked like mashed potatoes fall off onto the floor.

"Miles?" Nora asked.

"I am so sorry," Miles said.

The busboy put his hands up, and said, "I got it. Thanks."

"Miles?" Nora asked.

Her voice did something to Miles that he can't explain. All he knew was he had to stay calm and not react or overreact when he stood.

"Oh, hey. I didn't see you there," Miles said.

Nora's smile brightened not only the darkest corners of this place but also the darkest parts within Miles.

"What are you doing here?" Nora asked.

I was wrong. She didn't invite me. It doesn't matter. I'm here and she is here. Should we eat something? But not off the floor or the guy

"We talked about their famous hamburgers, and it made me hungry, so here I am," Miles said. What are you doing here?"

"Really? That was this like morning," Nora said.

She stood and picked a few spaghetti noodles that hung off my shoulder. Nora's nails were a deep shade of purple, which went well with her leather jacket. It crinkled and rubbed together as she tossed it into the busboy's bin. She smelled like raspberry lemonade.

"You definitely make an impression wherever you go, don't you?" Nora said.

No, but you do.

Over her shoulder, Nora's date walked toward them. His manicured nails were better than any man Miles had ever seen. He pushed up the sleeves of his royal blue sweater which revealed freshly shaved arms. He wasn't as fit as Nora.

He gave Nora a wink. Miles curled his bottom lip in disgust. Nora stepped to Miles's side as her date got closer. Her hand drifted down Miles's wrist and she laced her finger with Miles's. He wanted to look down, but didn't.

"Seriously, that bathroom is a disease waiting to happen. Hi. Who are you?" Todd asked.

Get a whiff of that. He must know Elana because my eyes are starting to sting from the bath of cologne he took.

Nora turned to introduce him to Miles.

"Todd. This is..." Nora said.

Nora tightened her grip on Miles's finger, which gave Miles gave her a confused look. She widened her eyes as if she couldn't think of answer. Finally, Miles took the hint.

"Miles. Nora's cousin," Miles said.

He unlaced his finger from Nora's and held his hand out to Todd.

"Nice to meet you," Todd said.

When they shook, Miles winced. For a guy in a blue sweater, khakis, and loafers, he was very strong. But the gel in his hair was too much.

Todd might want to stay away from the flame. Where a lighter when I need one.

"Miles was just telling me he hasn't eaten all day, and I thought he could join us," Nora said.

Miles was happy to see Todd was taken aback. Miles was thrilled to know Todd couldn't have her all to himself. Besides, Miles wouldn't let it happen.

"Oh, yeah sure. Please join us," Todd muttered.

Todd motioned for Nora to slide into the booth, but she stood and waited for him to do it. Todd sat next to one of the neon lights that burned above in the window. Nora plopped down beside him and Miles sat across from her. He settled into an awkward silence.

"What can I get ya?" the server asked as she appeared at the table's edge.

"I would like to get the vegan black bean burger with no bread, sweet potato fries, and water with a bowl of limes. Not lemons. Limes." Todd said.

Miles watched as the server jotted it down, and pointed her pencil at Nora.

"She will have the chicken salad with no chicken, cheese, or dressing because it's not healthy. So, bring another bowl of limes with one lemon. Extra lettuce and tomatoes. Oh, make the salad small. No, make it large. No, a medium. Small, let's go small," Todd said.

"Is that what you want, darlin'?" Flo asked Nora.

"Yes, she does," Todd blurted out as he handed her the menu.

"Yeah, that's fine. But instead of no chicken," Nora glanced at Todd then back to the server. She leaned on the table with her chin in hand and continued, "I would like a huge chuck of beef. As far as the cheese goes, make sure it's melted under and over the beef on the bun.

Miles held back his laugh as Nora turned her head and gave Todd a grin.

"I'll take the dressing but make sure it's mayo, ketchup, and tons of mustard oozing out the sides with extra lettuce and tomatoes. Add pickles and garlic. Lots of garlic. Forget the lemons and limes, I would rather have fries with chili and cheese smothered all over them," Nora said.

Flo smirked as she wrote everything down then glanced up at Todd for his reaction. Then she noticed Miles.

"And for you? Another glass of water?" Flo asked Miles.

"I'll have what she's having," Miles said as he pointed at Nora, who grinned and arched her eyebrows.

"You're going to clog your arteries up with all that grease and fat," Todd said as he polished his spoon with a small napkin.

"One can only hope. Right?" Nora said.

"If you don't mind my asking, but how close are y'all?" Todd asked after he gave up on cleaning.

"Oh, we're real close. Like *Flowers in the Attic* close." Nora said.

I didn't see that one coming. What a way to explain it. Todd isn't listening. I know because he's too busy cleaning off his section of the table.

"Yeah. Todd is close to his cousins the same way" Todd said.

Her laugh. I want to hear more of it. Todd has no clue what he said. But I do. It's our inside joke now. I like it. Here's a thought Nora, let's make more memories.

Together.

CHAPTER EIGHT

JESTER AND THE KNIGHT

With two to-go boxes, Miles watched as Nora and Todd talked. Miles was glad he stayed. Being the third wheel, as most people said, didn't exist. Hell, Todd didn't exist. Miles watched as Todd went in for a hug, but Nora stepped back. Todd wasn't as thrilled about that as Miles was. Nora walked toward Miles.

"Well, another date gone wrong. Darn," Nora said, her voice dripping with sarcasm.

Try to say something without smiling.

"I'm sorry," Miles said.

"I'm not. It was one of the best nights of my life. If it wasn't for you, I would have been bored out of my mind," Nora said.

Nora chuckled as she took the to-go boxes from Miles and tossed them into the trash as they began to walk.

"What were you doing with the douche in the first place?" Miles asked.

"Douche? I think you're giving him too much credit," Nora said.

"Then I take it back," Miles said.

"It was a blind date. Todd was my brother's college roommate. For some strange reason, he thought we would make an awesome couple. My brother's words, not mine," Nora said.

Clearly, her brother doesn't know her at all.

"Come on. The night is still young. Let's do something," Nora said.

Nora felt thrilled about anything and everything. The night was still young, and the quarter was just about to begin.

"Like what?" Miles asked.

"Anything. This is 'Nawlins. The Big Easy. The Crescent City. The city that never sleeps." Nora said.

"That's New York," Miles said.

"Ah, but there's a difference between us and New York," Nora said.

"And what's that?" Miles asked.

Nora took my hand and dragged me the rest of the way toward the French Quarter.

"Us," Nora said.

Laissez les bons temps rouler.

***

Nora rushed down the aisle, slid her fingers against the thousands of purples, greens, yellows, and so many other colored beads, then picked up a Mardi Gras mask. Red streaks were across the eyes, while exquisite feathers flowed around the curves of her face and showed her smile. *It fits her.* Bright and big, she lit up the room. She tossed Miles a matching mask, and he put it on. Shaking his head, he chose something more in his personal style. She squealed when he showed her the butterfly mask.

There are things about me that you might find wrong.

One by one, they tried on different masks and walked the aisles like they were on a runway. Nora modeled a silver and gold crescent moon. The one Miles liked more than any other was the devil mask. Nora shook her head, no. She stepped it up a notch, posing with a multi-colored cat mask with heavy whiskers. Miles put on a simple black mask with an oversized pirate hat with feathers as Nora clapped her hands as he strutted his stuff.

I have to tell you something.

***

They walked down Bourbon Street, passed crowds of people on night tours, listened to stories about New Orleans's haunted history. The tour guides were dressed in their best spooky costumes. Miles had the night he always wanted with someone who wanted to be with him. He wore a light-up jester hat that Nora talked him into. She brought something out in him he never thought existed.

Danica never did.

Danica was a mistake.

***

Danica's hand gripped the edge of the kitchen sink. She knocked over the glasses drying on the side and hit the faucet, turning on the water. Slowly, the sink filled as Miles waited for his moment.

Miles pressed his body against her back and held her head under the water. Bubbles engulfed the sink as she screamed and gasped for air. Miles was not going to let it happen. The bubbles grew smaller. Miles tightened his grip.

Eventually, she stopped.

Out of breath, Miles let go, and Danica dropped to the floor.

Dead.

***

Around every corner, street performers did their routines. The Man in Gold, as he was known, was a statue. Miles stood beside him and posed like a thinking man. Balance was not his friend and Nora circled as he stumbled.

Dressed as a skeleton, a man either leered or jumped at passerby's, which included Miles and Nora.

Don't hate me, Nora. It's called priority, and I wasn't one of them.

Nora grabbed Miles's hand and twirled herself in and out, then landed against Miles's body. *I've never met anyone like you. We have the same haunted past, but different faces. We have to be the same.*

"I have an idea," Nora said.

***

I have a haunted past, Nora. But you do too. Don't be afraid. You can open up to me about anything. I want you to tell me everything about yourself. Secrets, lies, anything.

Nora rubbed her arms. Miles pulled the snowy white blanket over their legs as they settled in for a carriage ride, the horse clicked, and the wheels turned. She lightly played with the blanket's fringe. The cold wind rushed through and blew the edges of her hair back. She took his arm and wrapped it over her shoulder, snuggling in close. At this exact moment, they were the only ones that existed. Nora grabbed his hand.

"Your hands are so warm," Nora said.

"You know what they say. Warm hands, cold heart," Miles said.

Let me warm you up.

She couldn't take her eyes away. They intertwined their fingers and eventually clasped hands. Miles hesitated his lean toward her. After he placed his hand against her cheek, he curled his fingers inside her hair and drew her into him.

"Miles?" Nora asked.

He kissed her hard and was passionate.

"Miles. The ride is over," Nora said.

Miles glanced around and saw the ride was over, and Nora stood by the carriage as people stared at him waiting to get on. I hopped off. They walked away and into the crowd on the other side of the street, near the painted wall.

"You did it again," Nora chuckled.

"Did what?" Miles asked.

"Go off in space. Where did or where do you go?" Nora asked.

"The ride was so relaxing. Guess I got carried away.," Miles said.

"Maybe next time you should take me with you. I would love to escape this place sometimes," Miles said.

"You always have an open invitation," Miles said.

"I might take you up on that offer," Nora said.

I would love it.

Nora stopped near Bourbon Street as people walked by. She sighed, and her chest rose and fell slowly as she swallowed hard.

I don't want this to end either. So, let's not let it. We can go anywhere. Do anything. Oh, the way she licks her lips. All I want to do is kiss her right now, right here. I want you to scream my name and wake the dead.

"Well, I guess I will see you around," Nora said.

"I'm sure we'll run into each other again," Miles said.

"Hopefully sooner rather than later," Nora snickered.

"I'm going with sooner. If you still want to help me with getting Petal Perfection out to the world. I was thinking of a website," Miles said.

I'm wondering if she assumed I'd forgotten. I was waiting for the perfect opportunity. You're relieved. I understand you didn't know how to approach me about it. I understand what you're saying. What you're saying makes sense to me. It would be strange after such a close call.

"I'll help you get it up," Nora said.

You have no idea, Nora.

"I'm glad we ran into each other," Nora said.

"Me too," Miles said.

No, don't leave. I just want a few more minutes with you.

"Nora," Miles said.

"Yeah?" Nora asked as she turned around.

Miles tossed her his jester hat. After she caught it, she put it on. Miles watched as she posed.

"How do I look?" Nora asked.

"Not bad. I make a better jester," Miles said.

Nora chuckled, and said, "You are something else, Miles Pike."

"Do you wanna see something?" Miles asked after a quiet moment fell over them

***

The purple color of the flower's petals faded to white as it bloomed. Miles stared as Nora examined it. He could tell she wanted to touch it, but she hesitated. He stood behind her near the shadowed wall as Nora stood and looked amongst the rows of flowers on the rooftop of Petal Perfection.

"What is this one called again?" Nora asked.

"It's called a viola," Miles said. "Meaning a purple pansy. It's a popular flower to plant. But it only blooms in the winter, spring, and summer."

The roof was filled with potted flowers, which were illuminated by small light bulbs that surrounded them, for when Miles worked at night. Miles thought Nora was the perfect flower to add to his collection as she stood in the middle of the flowers. She turned to him. Her smile made him nervous. She pointed at another flower.

"What's that one called?" Nora asked.

Miles glanced at the lance-shaped, grayish-colored leaves with a hint of green, and the clusters of petals ranged from blue to yellow to purple to white and pink to lavender.

"These are stock flowers. Florists use them for bouquets, flower arrangements, like for center pieces, and of course, people plant them," Miles said.

Nora turned to a row of orchids. They were a variety of colors. The stems of some of the plants were hanging low, while some were on the verge of coming out from their cocoons.

She pointed several more times. And Miles was happy to tell her everything.

"Peonies. They are old-fashioned. Most of the time, they are used for bridal bouquets. The pink ones symbolize happiness and romance. Double lilies are popular and perfect for table arrangements because they are clean and won't mess up a white tablecloth." Miles said.

He walked over to another row. Different layers of petals unfolded from the ball-like center to create an exquisite flower.

"Ranunculuses," Miles laid one in his hand. "Their beauty is completely unmatched."

"What about roses? They are what everyone wants," Nora said.

"Not true, I mean it's what people order on Valentine's Day, when it's someone's birthday. But there are so many others," Miles said.

He heard himself continue to list flowers and describe them, the season they grow in, and Nora hung on his every word. He watched her as she never took her eyes from him, especially his lips. He caught her as she bit on her lower lip. He became flabbergasted.

"Don't get me started on dandelions and daffodils," Miles said.

"All of them are so beautiful," Nora said as she glanced around.

"Nothing is as beautiful as this one," Miles said.

He knew Nora was interested when she leaned up and over. She had no choice but to approach Miles. He grinned, knelt down, and motioned her to do the same. In the middle of the row was a little bundle of skull-shaped flowers.

"I couldn't decide which you would like better, so I grew all of them," Miles said. "These are orchids, snapdragons. Baby orchids, mostly. But they're remarkable in that they resemble a person's skull. A bit morbid, but I think it's interesting."

"I never knew there were skull flowers. That it too cool," Nora said.

She stood from her bent knee. They came face-to-face. Inches separated them. The night's sky, the party lights, and the rows of flowers surrounded by spicy, sweet, jasmine, and vanilla scents made for a night to remember.

"Are you a secret botanist or something?" Nora asked.

Miles laughed.

"Or something," Miles shook his head, "I'm just a guy who loves his garden of girls," Miles said.

"Garden of girls," Nora looked across the rows of flowers, "I like that." Nora said.

The moment was right. Everything was perfect. Miles gazed into Nora's eyes. She wanted it as much as he did. He felt his heart leapt from his chest. But he knew it was time. A wind blew through and caught a strand of Nora's hair. He curled it within his fingers, then placed it behind her ear. He leaned in.

His phone rang. And he stopped.

He pulled it out, narrowed his eyes, and stepped back from Nora.

"Hello?" Miles asked.

He paused and listened to the person on the opposite line. The color in his face went pale, and his throat went so dry he couldn't remember to swallow as he forced out his next words.

"What do you mean Elana is missing?" Miles asked.

CHAPTER NINE

PRETENDING TO BE ME, BUT NOT ME

Miles watched Elana's dad as he stared into his half-filled glass of whiskey in the sunroom of the Stansbury house. It was bright and warm, yet somber at the same time. The drink in Mr. Stansbury's hand remained untouched. The constant tapping from another glass drew Miles's attention toward the window.

Chet, one of Elana's best friends from prep school, was outside. Miles didn't know him well and didn't particularly care about him either. He had a brief conversation with Chet during dinner one night, where Chet asked about the difference between a rose and the popularity of paper roses in recent months. After that lengthy two-hour discussion, Miles decided Chet wasn't his kind of person.

Fairy, Elana's other best friend, had her phone in hand since Miles arrived. She was bright and smart, though at times Miles didn't see it, he only heard about it from Elana. Most of the time, Fairy never lifted her head from her phone. She saw herself as a social media queen, or at least that was her belief, as she posted pictures with questionable fashion choices, and pictures of healthy, organic meals. But a genius at computers. She had made a virus in college and imported it into the university's computer system; she was expelled, then hired at one of the leading computer companies in the United States.

Miles waited when the silence broke.

"I don't think we should overreact," Miles said

Fairy perked up for the first time, and said, "I agree. This isn't the first time she has gone off the grid."

"True," Chet said. "Remember in school when that jock broke up with her? She walked out of school and directly into the woods. She didn't come back for three days."

"What did you do, Miles?" Fairy asked. She only disappears when she gets dumped."

Miles watched as Fairy and Chet stared at him.

"We didn't break up," Miles said. He noticed their glares. "We didn't. Look."

He pulled out his phone. He shared Elana and his recent texts. They were light, full of things like, *I love you. I miss you. Wish you were here. I'll see you in a few weeks.* Typical couple saying along with photos.

Mr. Stansbury took Miles's phone and flipped through Elana's texts.

"This is from a week ago, Sorry Miles. I'm just a little nervous. The post where she was supposed to check into told me she hadn't made it in yet," Mr. Stansbury said as he handed Miles back his phone.

"It' alright Mr. Stansbury. I understand," Miles said.

Miles couldn't imagine what Mr. Stansbury felt, but he felt equally worried. She had never gone completely dark before. He sent her a text that read, "Please text your dad and me when you can. We are so worried about you. I love you."

Then, he received a reply.

"She texted back," Miles said.

Chet walked over and yanked the phone from Miles's hand.

"No, she didn't. It wasn't delivered," Chet said.

"She must be out of the service area," Fairy suggested.

Mr. Stansbury poured himself another drink, downed it, and let out a long sigh.

"Let's give her a few more days. If she doesn't call any of us, I will get the police involved," Mr. Stansbury said.

The police? I hope you call me Elana.

CHAPTER TEN

ALL THE FLOWERS HAVE DIED

Miles bent down with a flower in his hand. Only a few petals clung to its broken stem. He stood. The flower shop was a wreck.

The windows with the shop name were broken from the inside out. Whoever it was, threw some of the larger vases through them, and they lay on their side, destroyed after they hit the ground.

Every flower had a place in the shop. Roses to the left. Lilies to the right with the marigolds and springs of baby's breath. The hydrangeas had a second of the wall to themselves. Miles made sure they were in a colorful pattern and in a pinwheel. The carnations that were so popular at prom time sat in the corner. There are between one hundred and forty-six to one hundred and fifty recognized species. Miles had seventy-five of them.

Now, all of them were shredded. The roses clipped off at the heads, the lilies plucked from their stems, and the hydrangea pinwheel turned too small, twisted knobs no one would want anymore. As far as the rest of the flowers in the shop, they wore the bottoms and designs of the shoes the burglars wore.

On either side of the shop the walls were smeared with various colors of spray paint. There were symbols but they didn't make sense, not to Miles, Davis, or even the police.

The police. They were useless. They chalked it up to some burglars who thought Miles had a safe in the back or a hidden locked box. He didn't. Also, the police said someone must have watched the shop for weeks before they struck, and Miles's schedule. They even knew when Davis left, because it happened when he was out.

Miles didn't believe that. This was something else. And he felt it deep inside.

"I am so sorry, Miles. I could have sworn I turned on the alarm," Davis said.

Miles nodded in agreement then turned toward the back where the counter was. The top of it was busted in. The police said it must have been with a sledgehammer, and that included the register. Inside there was about hundred and sixty dollars. Miles never kept more than that because most of the payments were called in and placed on debit along with credit cards.

"You should fire me. I suck," Davis said.

Miles noticed that something was on the floor. Something shiny.

"It was an accident, Davis. It could have happened to anyone. Even me," Miles said.

"Yeah, but it *didn't*," Davis said.

Miles bent down. The silver tip stuck out from underneath the counter's end. Miles pulled it out. It was a pen. A ballpoint pen. Morand Real Estate was etched in gold.

Son of a bitch.

CHAPTER ELEVEN

RESTAURANT WOES

Miles wasn't surprised when he received a call from Heathcliff Morand. He was happy to meet with him.

Miles walked into Roux, a fancy restaurant where they charge you an arm and a leg. And it should be, with all the awards and Michelin chefs they have employed over the last ten years. It was the most expensive restaurant in the city and famous for its spicy blood sausage boudin. The service, not so much.

Miles stood in front of the podium; he waited for the dimwitted greeter to acknowledge him, but he didn't. Most people who work here believe they are special. But Miles knew all they did was flash a fake smile and pray someone discovered them. Miles watched as the greeter turned, then looked him up and down. Miles knew the staffer judged him by the way he was dressed.

"Can I help you?" the greeter asked.

Condescending prick.

"I'm here to meet someone," Miles said.

"Here? You're meeting someone *here*?"

"Miles! Miles!" a loud voice called out.

Heathcliff waved like a madman and was louder than a screaming baby as Miles peered over the greeter's shoulder.

"Do you need me to walk you? Or can you manage not to bump the tables of paying customers?" the greeter asked.

"I can't promise anything," Miles said.

He made way to Heathcliff while the real estate magnate chugged his glass of wine, snapped to the server for another, and held up his empty glass.

Miles turned his body sideways as he tried to avoid the tables, but they were so close, he couldn't help but hit the edges, which annoyed the customers.

"Mr. Morand," Miles said.

"Heathcliff, please. Sit. Do you want anything?" Heathcliff asked.

"No thanks," Miles said.

"Nonsense," Heathcliff said. He hollered across the room to a server all in white with a red tray in his hand, "You. Hey, you. My friend needs a drink."

Friend? Where in the hell did that come from?

Embarrassed, the server rushed over as Mr. Stansbury wrapped his hand around another glass of red wine. It was amazing how much the human body can handle, as he drowned himself. Miles was reminded of Jenna.

***

"Oh, no you don't."

Miles grabbed Jenna by her long auburn hair right as she placed her hand on the back door. She kicked and screamed, but Miles didn't let go. He dragged her toward the bathroom. She dropped to her knees and hoped that it would stop her, but Miles was too strong. He stood her up every time.

"You've been a bad girl, Jenna," Miles said.

Miles was shocked when Jenna bit him. She bit down so hard that when Miles yanked his hand back, his blood coated her teeth and lips. Anger welled up in Miles. He punched her in the face. She fell backward. Miles checked his hand as Jenna rolled onto her stomach. He ogled her as he took a few steps and ended up above her. With her face towards the floor, Miles stomped on her legs and back. Jenna slowed to a crawl as Miles reared his leg back and kicked her in the back of the head, knocking her out.

In the bathroom, Miles dropped Jenna onto the floor. He scanned and landed his eyes on the tub. He turned on the water and plugged it into the rubber stopper. The slap from his hands on her shirt was loud as he pulled and bent her over the tub's edge. Jenna came to.

"No, don't," Jenna wailed as she placed, he hands on the tub, used all her strength to not go into the water. "I don't wanna die like my mother did," Jenna begged.

"You won't," Miles said.

From behind his back, Miles pulled out a long pair of scissors with a black handle. He watched the water turn pink to a reddish color as he sliced Jenna's throat.

"I love you so much," Miles said.

Miles stood over her as her face turned white, red, and her lips blue. Her blood dripped from her neck and slid into the white cracks on the tile. Miles lifted the scissors and saw her blood all over them. He grinned.

"Guess you should have done the dishes like I asked the other day," Miles said.

He opened and closed the scissors, then gestured to Jenna.

"Snip, snip, Jenna."

***

Miles took the white napkin from the water glass, and the server poured water inside it.

"What do you want?" Miles asked.

"Straight to business. I like that," Heathcliff said.

"Cut the shit Mr. Morand," Miles said.

The smile on Heathcliff's face faded, his brows lowered, and he cleared his throat. Miles was ready for anything he threw at him. Miles took the first sip of water. Through the glass, he never took his eyes off Heathcliff. He wanted to create as much tension as he could. The more uncomfortable, the better.

"Let me ask you a question," Heathcliff said.

"Let me ask you one," Miles said.

Heathcliff sat back in his chair, and said, "If that is how you want to play this, ask away."

"Where were you on Thursday night? Miles asked.

"Oh, I don't know. Maybe fucking my wife. Or my girlfriend. Who knows," Heathcliff said.

Miles watched Heathcliff as he diverted his stare from Miles and turned his head, an indication of guilt. But Miles had to hear it. Heathcliff returned his glare, more intense. Miles knew he wanted a challenge. Miles gave him one. Miles tossed the pen he found in his shop onto the table. Heathcliff picked it up.

"So that's where it went," Heathcliff said as he placed it inside his jacket pocket.

"Do you think it's funny to trash my shop?" Miles asked.

"No. It's not funny. But it sure was entertaining. I really loved the way the roses were snipped at the head. It reminded me of all those who went against me and lost," Heathcliff said.

"I wonder what the police are going to think," Miles said, standing up.

"Sit back down," Heathcliff said.

"Fuck you, Heathcliff," Miles said as he turned halfway to leave.

"I would sit down unless you want these to make front page news and be Channel Eight's six o'clock spotlight," Heathcliff said.

He dropped a manila folder on the dinner plate in front of Miles. He picked up the folder and pulled out a photo of himself. It was a shot of him on the lake late at night.

He had me followed.

Miles flipped through the pictures. Each one was a shot of him in different positions: the rowboat, him as he looked in different directions, him as he bent down over the side of the rowboat, and on land as he walked away.

Miles dropped back down into his chair. He glanced once more at the pictures and tossed them back at Heathcliff. Miles watched as he went through them.

"I see you got my good side," Miles said.

"I know it doesn't seem like much. And you want to call the police. So, I think they might find this interesting," Heathcliff said.

Miles jerked one of the pictures and stared at it. He didn't see what Heathcliff meant.

"It in the corner of the rowboat. The left corner if I'm correct," Heathcliff said.

Miles squinted. In the rowboat's floor to the left in the corner were small black pieces.

"Now I don't want to assume anything. But those are pieces of a garbage bag. I could careless, but a cop...well, they might find it interesting," Heathcliff said.

"Do you know how many people use the boats to go onto the water? A lot of people," Miles said.

"I agree with you. And they could have come from anywhere, from anyone. But you did use it," Heathcliff said.

"You're insane. It's nothing," Miles said.

Heathcliff laughed. Miles smiled. But underneath the table, Miles had a butter knife in his hand. He rubbed his finger up and down the sharp edges. He could use it. It wasn't as sharp as he would have liked, but still. He could jam it into Heathcliff's gut. The slice would be slow, but it would satisfy Miles.

"If it was nothing, you wouldn't have sat back down," Heathcliff said.

"Name it," Miles said.

Heathcliff pointed at Miles and said, "I knew it *was* something. What are you hiding, Miles?"

"Fucking name, it, Morand," Miles said.

Miles was shocked when Heathcliff slammed his fist on the table. It shook the glass and made the plates rattle. People glanced their way. Miles heard Heathcliff's voice, low and coming through gritted teeth.

"Do you think I came into my wealth and own all this land by being a nice guy? I make deals where they benefit me. I will dig so deep into your life to find something. I will – I know there's something. And when I find it and will use it to my advantage," Heathcliff said.

Miles knew Heathcliff was serious. He knew what was dug up would be awful, especially from Miles's past. It wasn't all roses. He had a lot of thorns. Sharp, embedded thorns. Miles knew there was only one thing to do.

"What's your offer?" Miles asked.

"A trade," Heathcliff said.

"Pictures for the flower shop. No catches. No lies. Just a clean sign over to me, and you do whatever you want. Go whatever you want. I don't give a fuck," Heathcliff said. "Oh, and one more thing."

Heathcliff held up a small black USB drive. Miles focused on it, and everything around him blurred. He couldn't hear anything except for deep, slow voices. He knew that if he didn't get it, his world would be in danger, which included his garden of girls. He wasn't going to have them plucked after all these years. Heathcliff wrapped his hand around the USB drive and placed it in his jacket pocket.

"Think about it," Heathcliff said.

"Sure," Miles said.

Miles rose from the chair. He turned his back as Heathcliff snapped his finger to the server. Miles figured it was for another glass of wine. Miles guessed threats made him thirsty. Then it hit him.

"What would you do to have it?" Miles asked.

"What?" Heathcliff asked.

And he turned around.

"What would you do to own my shop? Miles asked.

"I would do anything," Heathcliff said.

"Even commit murder," Miles said.

"If I had to," Heathcliff said.

That's all I needed to hear.

CHAPTER TWELVE

CATCH ME, KILL ME, OR SHOULD I DO THAT TO YOU?

Miles hurried down the street. His mind raced with thoughts. And he came down with one that he hated.

I'll have to burn it down. It's the only way.

No, he couldn't do that. Miles loved his special place. If he burned it all down, that could lead to a disaster, or at the very least, he would have to close the doors due to the lack of customers. Income to pay the bills barely came in. He couldn't even pay Davis, who was more than happy to do his job for free. Miles wondered *how long that was going to last.*

There had to be a way to get Heathcliff off his trail. But that USB drive was a problem. Miles knew he had to get his hands on it.

Good thing the pictures didn't show anything that could send him away. Whoever took them was at least ten to twenty minutes late.

Miles was eased at that thought. But what if Heathcliff did good on his threat? He would do anything, and Miles knew.

What if he already knows about my garden? What if someone had already seen his exes? What if that's on the drive? I have to have that USB drive.

Miles's phone rang. He took it out and saw Fairy's number.

"Hello?" he answered.

On the other end, Fairy's voice was a mix of excitement, seriousness, and nervousness, leaving Miles uncertain about her tone.

"Miles, it's Fairy," she said.

"It's a bad time right now. Can I call you back later?" Miles asked.

"I think I found Elana," Fairy replied.

Miles stood frozen in a busy spot on the sidewalk, people bustling around him.

"W-what do you mean you found her?" Miles stammered.

"I found her. She's in town," Fairy said. "Or at least, I think she is."

"Is she or isn't she, Fairy?" Miles pressed. There was a long pause. "Fairy?"

"The signal is going in and out, but she is definitely in New Orleans. I'm going to get her," Fairy said.

Miles's eyes widened, and he became over-stimulated and very loud.

"No, wait. Take me with you!" Miles exclaimed. "I have to see her."

"Okay, meet me tonight near the levee," Fairy instructed.

Miles semi-puffed out his cheeks, and tosses his head back, and said, "I'll be there."

Miles hung up, felt sick to his stomach, lost, scared, and excited all at once.

This day keeps getting better and better.

Miles wiped sweat off his forehead. He felt his pulse race and tightness invade his chest. He was sure he was about to be taken out by a heart attack or at least a major panic attack. He bent over and ended up on the wall right beside him. He leaned on it with his head between his legs. Then, his phone rang. He ignored it as he breathed in and out. It rang again. The vibration tickled his hand. So, he picked it up fast.

"Fairy, I will see you..." Miles said.

Who is this?

Miles pulled the phone from his ear only to see the caller ID was an unknown number. He stood.

"Mr. Pike?" a man asked.

"Uh, yeah. Can I help you?" Mile asked.

"I'm Private Investigator Leslie Chamberlin. I have been hired to find Elana Stansbury," Leslie said.

"Yes. I remember Mr. Stansbury saying he hired someone," Miles said.

Miles rocked back and forth as he listened.

"I was hoping we could get together and speak. When are you free?" Leslie asked.

Miles ran his fingers through his hair. He had to think of something. He had to keep his nose clean and his name out of this man's mind; he had to prevent himself from being looked at as a suspect. Elana was *missing*, not dead.

"I don't know. I've been working all morning, so ..." Miles said.

"I understand. Look to your left by the black iron fence," Leslie said.

Miles shifted his eyes over the bust streets, and sidewalks. Past the artist selling their pieces, the music played in the corner of the quarter, and through the kindergarteners on a field trip, Miles spotted Leslie.

Leslie Chamberlin was a handsome, tall man who was fondness for the color black and his hair was perfect with waves. He was nothing what he imagined he would look like, especially from the late night black and white detective shows he watched on television. Miles waved back as Leslie shook his hand over the tall crowd. Miles had no choice and headed over to Leslie, who stood near a beignet food cart.

"Nice to meet you. Mr. Stansbury mentioned he hired a P.I. Personally, I'm happy. Anything to bring Elana home."

Did he just do a quick package check? Yep, he did. Hey, pal! Eyes up here. Well, this is going to be easier than I thought. Welcome to charm city, Leslie.

They walked down the middle of the street as the through crowd grew, and they talked. The more Leslie flirts, the more Miles thinks this might be a way to get him off my ass. *Sorry, Leslie – you're not my type.*

"I have already talked with Mr. Stansbury, and he was in a meeting the day Elana disappeared," Leslie said.

Good to know.

"Oh, so you know the day she disappeared. I didn't know there was an actual date," Miles said.

"Well, it's just a working date as I like to say. I am basing all of this on the last time I believe she tested everyone," Leslie said.

Miles realized it must have been the first time Leslie had ever been to New Orleans. He was so interested in everything from the painters and local artists on the sidewalks to the fortunate tellers with plastic crystal balls, to the tourists that were seen as the eyes allowed,

"I talked to a few people, and I have learned she wasn't alone. Oblivious, but the other hikers said they never saw her. Don't you find that strange?" Leslie asked.

I know I'm not that good. He's freely sharing information to see my reaction. Smart, but not that smart.

"I wish I could help you, but Elana never really talked to me about hiking. It's not really my thing. I mean I did it for her. She's gone so much on the trail for work, I never missed a chance to be with her," Miles said.

"Where were you on the sixth?" Leslie asked.

Miles acted like he was thinking, He had no clue where he was. But there was an answer he could prove. They entered the line to the Beignet Truck.

"I was delivering flower orders all day," Miles said. "I'm always delivering flowers."

"And you can verify this?" Leslie asked.

At the front of the line, Leslie ordered a few beignets, since he had never had one before,

"Four beignets, please?" Leslie asked. He fiddled with his hat as she glanced up at Miles. "I should lie and won't. I received a copy of your flower delivery schedule. I saw a few weren't delivered."

Davis.

"There are those times. But I assure you I gave the customer a refund," Miles said.

"I also saw where your shop was wrecked. I'm so sorry to hear that," Leslie said with a mouth full of pastry and powdered sugar around the corners of his mouth. "Any leads?"

"Unfortunately, no. The neighborhood hasn't been the same since most of the businesses have shut down," Miles said.

Oh, please, you already know that. You wanted to know if I was going to mess up. Sorry. I know it better than an actor knows a script. Improvisation is not an option. Unless it's grabbing something and

smashing it over someone's head because they lied and cheated on you. With a fucking asshole.

"These are the best things I have ever had," Leslie said as he licked the sugar off his finger. "A little messy."

I think I'm gonna be sick.

"Best in town," Miles said.

"You seem like a straight-up guy. Plus, there's nothing in your story I can poke a hole in. But I do have to ask a few things. I think you might be able to help me out," Leslie said.

"Ask me anything," Miles said.

"How well do you know Fairy," Leslie asked.

"Fairy? She's Elana's best friend since prep school, from a rich family, twin sister to Chet," Miles said.

"Did Elana ever mention having problems with Fairy?" Leslie asked.

Leslie took out his small notepad and pen took notes on what he thinks I have an answer. At this point, I could make it up and this guy would believe it.

"No. She never talked bad or good about her. Why?" Miles asked.

"Elana and Fairy had a bad argument a week before I suspect Elana disappeared. And over texts which are completely telling," Leslie said.

I'll be damned. I didn't know that. She never mentioned that. But it's not like I gave her a chance either.

"She never mentioned having any problems with Fairy," Miles said.

So much for pretending. I don't have to play stupid. Please tell me more.

"I really shouldn't tell you. But I have already cleared you," Leslie said.

Are you serious? Already cleared me. You suck as a P.I.

"Well, that's a relief," Miles said.

"She and Elana had a relationship. A sexual relationship since they were in school. Elana broke it off and Fairy was upset. But she threatened Elana. And now she's missing. Consequence? I don't think so," Leslie said. "I'm so sorry you have to hear this on a day like today. I know this is hard for you as is."

You have no idea.

"It is. I planned on proposing to her when she finished this trip. I hope I still get to. You're just doing your job," Miles said.

Maybe you're not that bad at it. No, you are. You really are. Now to add a little something-something.

Miles lowered his head. He pinched the corners of his eyes near the nose and tried to hold it together.

"I didn't want to mention this– no, never mind. It's probably nothing," Miles said.

Leslie leaned forward, intrigued, and pen ready to write as he said, "No, please. Any information would be great."

Miles lowered his head to draw Leslie closer and spoke in a hushed tone, as if someone were nearby. Leslie glanced around and leaned closely in.

"I have been a little on edge and sometimes it feels like someone is following me. My shop is broken into too, Elana hasn't contacted me, and now you tell me Fairy might have something to do with this. Honestly, I'm starting to get a little scared," Miles said.

"I understand your concerns," Leslie said.

Miles sniffed a few times and said, "I just really miss her. I love her so much."

Leslie placed his hand on Miles's shoulder, and said, "Don't be hard on yourself. I'll investigate everything you mentioned. Look, we will find her. Her father mentioned she likes to go off the grid at times. I bet she's laying low and offline to take some personal time. It happened before to other family and friends. Hang in there and I will call you in a few days," Leslie said.

"Please feel free to contact me or come by the flower shop whenever you need to," Miles replied through a fake choke s if he was about to burst out in tears.

"I might take you up on that Mr. Pike," Leslie said.

Leslie placed his hand on top of Miles's, and looked at him. *Wow. I'm doing better than I thought.*

"I will see in soon," Leslie said.

"How soon? I would hate to not be able to talk or help you," Miles said.

"I'll check back in a few days," Leslie said."

"I look forward to it," Miles said.

Miles watched as Leslie walked away and eventually disappeared into the crowd. He knew two things: Leslie was going to be a pain for him, but he was also his partner in crime. One thing Miles was certain of was that he wasn't lying—someone had been following him. Maybe this was his chance to flush them out and use this to his advantage. Put Leslie on the path of Heathcliff.

Miles made his way to his shop, when he saw Nora as she stood outside on the phone. He instantly smiled as she did when she saw him. She waved at him and then hung up the phone.

"Look what the cat finally dragged in," Nora said. "Couldn't get out of bed today?"

"Didn't want to," Miles said.

Nora's body glistened under the late morning sun. She smelled great. *Like always.*

"To what do I owe this visit?" Miles asked.

"I wanted to invite you to a little thing tomorrow. It's nothing big, just a barbeque," Nora said.

It's a date.

"I would love to," Miles said.

Nora began to walk away, and she held up her phone.

"Great. I will call you with some details. Oh, and Miles, bring some of those flowers. You'll score big time with those."

With who?

CHAPTER THIRTEEN

FLIGHT OF THE FAIRY

Miles listened to the rain pelts on the hood of Fairy's car, all he could do was wait to see what she had to say. Her make-up was runny, and black streaks lightly lined her heavy-set cheeks, along with the red lipstick around most of the outer parts of her lips.

Yep, she's wasted. great. I knew I shouldn't have some or meet in a different place. Too late now.

Her pale skin was wrapped in black sleeves; her hair is lazily thrown into a messy ponytail with crimped strands hanging down. She looked like a poorly styled Barbie doll.

"What are we doing here, Fairy?" Miles asked.

Fairy dug inside the big black bag in her lap and tossed everything out into the backseat. Wallet, brush, another wallet, cellphone – Miles wasn't surprised when she needed another cigarette. Miles hated smoking. It was one of his rules: no smoking.

"Like I said on the phone I think I found Elana," Fairy said.

She finished her first cigarette, threw it out the window, and pulled out another.

"What do you mean you *think* you found her?" Miles asked.

She pulled out her phone and scrolled through the apps.

"I know it sounds strange but her and I have always known where each other is. I mean we're best friends. Besides it was like insurance," Fairy said.

Insurance? What kind of fucked up friendship did they have?

"Anyway. Her phone disappeared about a week ago, then reappeared three days ago. I have been tracking it, and it led me to…you," Fairy said.

Miles's heart dropped to his feet. Fairy showed the red line from the Appalachian Trail to him. Or rather behind Petal Perfection. The lake. Miles knew he had to think fast and close this chapter before it got out of hand.

"I went out to the lakeside the other night. I didn't see anything. Fuck, I didn't even know what I was looking for. But I know she's here. *There*," Fairy said.

Fairy clicked her lighter, but the wick wasn't working. She tried a few more times as Miles stared into the void. He didn't know what to do or say. He knew she wanted a reason why Elana's location was in my area. He had to act fast.

"Tomorrow morning, I'm going to contact the PI Mr. Stansbury hired. He would have more of a chance to get some search parties or at least some scuba divers. What if something happened to her?" Fairy asked.

"Let's just breathe. We can't be certain that app knows her location," Miles said.

Fairy leaned over the center console. He knew he had offended her, making her feel belittled, as if he thought she was stupid—or at least that the app was. He didn't realize how much she relied on technology to find Elana. Upset, she turned on her car.

"Fairy…"

"Some boyfriend you are. I don't think you even care she's missing. All you care about is that photographer," Fairy said.

"How do you know about her?" Miles asked.

"Please. I have been following since that day at Mr. Stansbury's house. The second you pulled out your phone and read out those texts, I knew something was wrong. I did a little digging, Miles. Did you know anyone can download a texting app," Fairy said.

In that moment, the monster within Miles awakened, craving blood. He knew he had to protect Nora at all costs.

"You know what? I think I will go to the police. They need…" Fairy said.

She never finished her sentence.

Miles slammed Fairy's head with as much force as I possible into the steering wheel. It wasn't enough to knock her out, but Miles felt glee. Especially after her blood spilled from her nose and mouth. He slammed her harder with each hit. Then on good measure, Miles angled and slammed her head onto the Eightball shifter. As she tried to open the door, her hand missed the door handle. Miles reared her head when she became so dazed she had no clue where she was.

She groaned. She attempted to touch her face and head, but she couldn't find it. She was so out of it. Miles watched her. He was slowing his anger down,

Miles could let Fairy go. It was too late for her. Miles reared back and punched her in the throat, hard. Then twice in the face. Finally, she passed out. Her head landed on the steering wheel and the horn blared. Miles was very thankful, no one else was around because the horn was so loud, he swore he heard a crack.

Here's hoping for the best.

He pushed her backward in the driver's seat, her mouth opened, and blood seeped from the corners of her mouth..

"So, what now?" a voice asked from the backseat.

Mom sat in the backseat and curiously filed her fingernails and waited for Miles to have a lightbulb moment. But nothing happened. If she would have kept her nose out and mouth shut – none if this would be happening.

"I'm thinking," Miles said.

"I would think harder," Mom said. Miles's mom leaned forward to Fairy, and said, "See there. She's still breathing."

"I know that," Miles said through gritted teeth "Just let me fucking think, mom."

He massaged his temples and stared out the window into the darkness. He usually had a plan. *Good one, Miles. Good one.* He winged it.

"Don't take that tone with me, young man," Mom said.

Miles knew she hated when he had a tone.

"Who names their child 'Fairy?'" Mom asked.

"I don't know her parents," Miles said.

"You have to get rid of her. Tonight,' mom said.

Miles turned to his mom in the backseat. Her glare was straight forward and spoke for her. Miles got out of the car, walked around, and opened the driver's side door. Fairy's body fell out. Miles looked around just to make sure, then pulled the rest of her out by her arms. Miles opened the trunk of Fairy's car, and dumped her inside. He stared down as his mom appeared beside him. She placed her hand on his shoulder.

"The lake," mom said.

"Like mother, like son."

Miles hit the gas and accelerated backward, laughing.

***

Through the beastly black night, Miles dragged Fairy's body through the sticky and slimy mud.

"I would help, but I just did my nails.," mom said, showing off her freshly manicured nails

Perfect timing as usual. And leaning against a tree, it's not like I'm struggling over here.

"Thanks, mom. How about you keep a lookout?" Miles said.

"I can do that. She deserved it," mom said.

"I didn't kill her and I overreacted," Miles said.

Underneath Fairy mud and wet leaves gathered. The ends of her hair became coated, and the blood continued to dry on her face as the night's air hit it.

"Can you believe she mentioned Nora?" Miles asked.

"I like her. She gives you a run for your money," mom said.

Miles dropped Fairy's legs.

"I know. I have never met anyone like her before, mom," Miles said.

Miles saw the look on his mom's face. She was proud. Proud he finally met someone who understood him. All she ever wanted was for him to find love, and devotion. She smiled at him as she embraced him.

"I just want you to be happy. If it's with Nora, then it's with her. I support you all the way," mom said.

"I am. She means a lot to me," Miles said.

Fairy began to moan softly. She was slow to wake up, but eventually, she would, and who knows who might hear her as she screamed at the top of her lungs? Miles' mom saw her.

"We have a problem.," mom said.

"Damnit," Miles said.

"I guess you should have taken care of her in the car," mom said. "She looks like one of those stuffed animals in those claw machines. Pick on up and it slips – she looks like the animal that has been dropped a million times," mom said.

"I'll take care of it," Miles said.

"Oh honey. I think you better hurry. I think the little trash hole is actually going to wake up. Is it wrong I'm so excited if she sees what's coming to her?" Mom asked. She clapped with excitement. "Oh, this is such a rush. What's your plan?"

"Not the plan, more like a detour," Miles said. "I can fix this."

Miles glanced around, his eyes landed on a rock a few feet away. He rushed up and grabbed it. Miles thought, *this ought to do it*. When he stepped back beside his mom, he lifted the rock above his head.

Before he did anything, Miles stared at Fairy.

She's always been an obstacle.

He raised the rock a little higher. His heart pounded. He had rules. He had reasons. Fairy was nothing to him and here he was about to kill an innocent person. He searched his mind for a reason and came up with nothing.

"Wait!" mom said.

"What?" Miles asked.

"Flowers. You need to give Nora the biggest, best, and most amazing bouquet you have ever made. Maybe throw in a little note saying something like, hey or thinking about you, it will work," mom said.

"Not a bad idea. Ooooh, dinner," Miles suggested.

"Yessss... She will love it. But make sure there are not any nails sticking out of the walls like it was with," mom thinks for a minute, and continues, "Oh I can't remember her name. There's been so many," mom said.

Miles looked down on time and saw Fairy open her eyes.

"Hello, Fairy," Miles said.

Miles slammed the rock down repeatedly. He couldn't stop. The adrenaline throughout his body pumped. The rock was weightless as he continued to pummel her. All Miles could see was Nora with her arms wrapped around him, tight.

After a few hits, Fairy went limp. He dropped the rock.

"Goodbye, Fairy."

CHAPTER FOURTEEN

MISSING PERSON

When they said it takes a village to raise a child, they never mentioned it takes one to find one. In this case, Elana.

Over the last few weeks, Miles learned about tracking, locations, and geotags. He had no choice. He wished he had asked Fairy more and better in-depth questions before he killed her. But he didn't. And now he learned the hard way.

What surprised Miles was how Fairy didn't have a lock on her phone. All he did was swipe up, and there was her whole world. One twisted and sick world. More than anything, he learned she had Elana's location, and it was behind the flower shop.

Since Miles had Elana's phone, all he had to do was change the location from New Orleans to the Appalachian Trail, where Elana had been before she came back for a fun and wild weekend with that guy.

But the problem was he didn't know if it was going to work. Or invite the police to his doorstep.

Miles should have been there. He would have acted the part of the grieving boyfriend better than anyone. Yet, he wasn't there. Miles watched as Mr. Stansbury stood at the opening of just one of the Appalachian Trails as he gave an emotional speech.

"We just want our beloved Elana back safe and sound from the nature she so dearly loves," Mr. Stansbury said.

I can't believe all these people are here. Most are probably here because A) Mr. Stansbury has something on them, like money or an extended contract, or B) they want to be part of the in-crowd. When Mr. Stansbury said he'd spare no expense, he meant it. You would think the whole country was shut down. The city did. Look at him.

Miles hated to think about it, but people go missing from the trails all the time. In total, the Appalachian Trail covered over two thousand miles and crossed many states. Elana knew that when she stepped foot on it. Finding her would be like finding a needle in a haystack.

Yet there were people there, and they waited for the chance to search for it. But they didn't know she wasn't there. Miles turned the volume up a little. Chet stepped in and had a few words to say.

This should be good.

"We had a close friendship, and I want to say that I am not going to give up until I find her," Chet said.

Mr. Stansbury, Chet, searchers and police were there, but where is Fairy? Miles had heard mutters of Fairy's name in a few conversations by some of the police. Just then a police detective stepped in for Mr. Stansbury as he wept.

"Good morning, ladies and gentlemen. I wanted to tell you and Mr. Stansbury that I and the rest of the team, along with volunteers, will not stop until we bring Elana home," the detective said.

The trail spanned over 2,190 miles, which made it one of the longest and most challenging trails, from Springer Mountain in Georgia to Mount Katahdin in Maine, and it passed through fourteen states. And that didn't include the wild animals they might encounter and other hikers who, for whatever reason, may or may not talk with them. The possibly abandoned campsites—they were going to find someone or something, but it wasn't going to be Elana.

"What about the boyfriend?" a reporter asked.

Miles's eyes slide to the reporter. He knew someone was going to mention him at some point. He didn't expect it right before the search started. He knew he needed to stay calm, cool, but he needed to look scared, confused, and anxious to start looking for her.

"I will answer all question in due time. Look, guys. I have no clue what has happened to her. All I know is that we have a missing hiker, and the longer I stand here, the more she is in there per her posts in social media," the detective said as he pointed behind him at the trail.

Miles's phone rang. It was Leslie, the private investigator.

"Leslie, so good to hear from you," Miles said.

"Hey Miles. I just wanted to give you an update on what is happening with Elana's case," Leslie said. "We have a suspect. But that's all I can say. But I think you can figure it out on your own just by who was at the interview," Leslie said.

As long as it's not me. I have tried to cover my tracks.

"Is there anything I can do? Don't hesitate to call," Miles said.

That was easy. Fairy flies the coop, and here I am sitting pretty. What could ruin this day?

"Do you think her picture will be on milk cartons?" A man's voice said.

Miles turned to his right, and Heathcliff stood with his eyes glued to the TV and a picture of Elana.

"I don't think they do that anymore," Miles said.

"She was pretty," Heathcliff said.

Was. What an odd choice of words.

"What do you want?" Miles asked.

"I was just checking in on my place," Heathcliff said.

"*Your* place? Interesting. I could have sworn I told you no a few weeks ago," Miles said.

"Things in my area of work can change on a dime. Besides, I want to up the ante on that little deal of ours."

"We don't have a deal," Miles said.

Heathcliff laughed Miles off and said, "I've been digging around and saw that you took a second mortgage out on this place a few years ago. And saw the outstanding balance. I offered the bank the full payment."

Miles knew he couldn't do that. Miles owned the building. Then it hit him. Heathcliff must have gotten the bank information the night he trashed the shop. Illegal as hell, but Miles commended him for never backing down. It wasn't like he had never done worse.

"They have accepted it," Heathcliff said. "Consider it a gift."

A gift would be if you dropped dead on the floor with a stapler lodged deep in your throat and I ate a peanut butter and jelly sandwich as you choked on it.

"You can take your gift and blow it out your ass," Miles said.

Heathcliff laughed. He wagged his finger like he was scolding a child, then proceeded to the door.

"Now is that any way to talk to someone who just saved your ass from going under?" Heathcliff asked.

Going under with blocks on each foot is the best idea Heathcliff has ever offered. I accept.

CHAPTER FIFTEEN

HOT DOGS AND MURDER

Nora parked her car and Miles glanced out the passenger side window.

"Here we are," Nora said.

Miles saw the glee written all over her face.

"And *where* is here?" Mile asked.

Nora opened her door, and said, "Get ready for the time of your life!"

Miles didn't know what that meant, but if Nora was there, then it would be an amazing day. He got out and walked a few feet behind Nira.

"This is the place dreams are made of," Nora said as she twirled around.

It was a house in the middle of suburbia down by the French Quarter, nestled between two large brick buildings that were currently unoccupied. It was an old-style French cottage, with blue steps that led through a black iron gate and to a long porch. The French doors resembled stain glass windows, the sunlight reflected off and made the most amazing patterns. Miles could have watched the color changes all day. They're not the choice he would have picked for outdoor plants, for this particular house, but they were easy to maintain. The house's color was a clean teal. Miles knew someone took pride in their house because he never saw one mark on the outer walls. The old-styled black streetlamps were embedded on the side with flames lit.

Miles stopped when he saw a familiar face. On the sold sign next door was Heathcliff.

I can't get away from this guy.

Vampires, ghosts, and demons—New Orleans was a haunted city, and Miles would have preferred to encounter one of them instead of dealing with Heathcliff as a nuisance. Nora slipped her arm through Miles's.

"Fuck that guy. We are here for fun, not assholes," Nora said.

"I'm all for fun," Miles said.

He knew he had a sarcastic tone, and Nora caught it. She leaned back and said, "Yeah, fun."

Nora let go of Miles, and he watched as she stepped into the house's bushes, and not the vacant house's yard. Miles watched as Nora kicked Heathcliff's sign down. Then she stomped on him like he was right there. She huffed and puffed. Miles saw she enjoyed it. A lot. Her hair flew in the makeshift wind, her hands turned into fists, and the heel of boot started to split the sign and busted a hole right in Heathcliff's face. Miles listened as she talked to Heathcliff like he was there.

Miles couldn't believe he watched this.

How did I get so lucky?

"Go fuck yourself you piece of shit," Nora said with every stomp.

Done, Nora fixed her hair and placed it back in place. She straightened her clothes and pulled down on her jacket until the wrinkles were out. She took a deep breath and blew it out loud that Miles heard it. She stepped back over the bushes, and Miles was in awe.

"I don't know what to say," Miles said.

"Fucker deserved it," Nora said.

They laughed. She gripped Miles by the hand and pulled him toward the house. They went up some steps and stood in front of the French doors.

"Pick a door, any door," Nora said.

Miles was about to pick the left one but hesitated. Picked the door on the right.

"Wrong," Nora said. "It's this one," Nora said as she opened the other door.

"Guess I should have gone with my gut," Miles said.

"I smell bullshit. I saw you hesitate," Nora said as she latches her finger under the hidden flat knob and pulls it out.

"I don't what you are talking about," Miles said.

"Yeah, right," Nora said as she shoved Miles inside.

She can read me so well.

CHAPTER SIXTEEN

HUNGRY ANYONE?

The home was bigger on the inside than the outside.

The foyer was bright white, with cherry wood floors and flowers on either side. Miles cracked a smile at the flower arrangements. In one antique green vase, rustic cotton stalks interlocked with purplish-blue Galaxy Orchid Stems. They were healthy and received just the right amount of water and sunlight, which made them bloom large and full. On the other side, in a curved stand, a bundle of simple long-stemmed branches with small red berries flourished and hung over the edge of the clear, wide empty vase, which had a red cloth ribbon tied around it.

Clean, concise, and colorful, just the way he would have made them to be. Miles needed to meet the person who was responsible for the beautiful foyer aesthetic. I already knew them. They had an intense love for décor. A long hallway with a half-open door and a steep staircase on the right that winds around to the left, where the bedrooms are, was in front of him. Miles slid his eyes across the pictures lined the walls beside the banister.

"This place is amazing," Miles exclaimed.

Nora grabbed his hands and pulled him to some of the pictures on the wall, especially a picture of a child dressed as Michael Myers as the clown from *Halloween*. Choppy bangs hung over the white mask and red nose. The collar was lacy and frilly as the clown suit was dripped in blue, yellow, and red. They held a plastic butcher knife.

"Guess," Nora said.

"Is that you?" Miles asked ass pointed at the picture.

"Every year. The moment I saw *Halloween* I became obsessed. The original, not the remake. Although I've seen and own all of them."

I was Jason from Friday the 13th.

"Cute," Miles shrugged.

"Cute. I'm not supposed to be cute. I was supposed to be scary. Blood-chilling. At least that's what my brothers said. I would chase them around the house practicing stabbing for when I went trick-or-treating," Nora said.

I love and admire your passion, Nora. I'll let you stab me anytime. Can I stab you? It will be spine bending.

"Oh, I can see it. Yeah, now I'm feeling it," Miles said.

Nora gave a half-smile and shook her head. They still held each other's hands. She lowered her gaze. They laced their fingers even more tightly.

This is the moment I've been looking forward to. Damnit, I need a breath check. I don't wanna mess this up with bad breath. Show me the bathroom and I promise the raid for mouthwash will be quick, Nora.

"I have more pictures upstairs if you're interested in taking a look," Nora said.

Fuck the mouthwash.

"I would love to see them," Miles said.

"Nora is that you?" A female voice shouted with a French-creole accent.

"Mom?" Nora said.

Nora dropped Miles's hand and walked to the center of the foyer, where her mother entered, from the kitchen as she wiped her hands on a yellow towel. Miles saw where Nora got her looks. Her mom was tall and slender with long brown hair in a braid which draped over her right shoulder. Miles watched as they embraced tightly.

Nora's mom cupped her cheeks and smiled at her like she hadn't seen her in years. Miles felt their bond in the air. It was strong, just like Nora.

"Mom. I want you to meet someone. This is Miles Pike," Nora said.

"Nice to meet you, Mrs. Asher," Miles said.

Nora's mom took it with force. Miles was shocked. She didn't just have a strong bond with Nora; she was as strong physically like Nora as well.

"You're right fille. He is handsome. It's very nice to meet you too. And please call me Kelly," she said.

Nora blushed as Kelly threw the dish towel over her shoulder. She never took her eyes off Miles. He knew Kelly was sizing him up. She wanted to make sure Miles was right for her little girl. After all, Miles now knew, she talked about him, which was a good sign and a huge step in their relationship. But that also meant they knew about Elana, and about the search.

"Could I talk to you for a minute, fille?" Kelly said toward Nora.

Here it comes. The stare. The questions. The 'he shouldn't be here because his girlfriend didn't come back from her hike' feelings.

"Should I leave?" Miles asked.

That took Kelly and Nora off guard and Miles knew it would. He stood there with puppy dog eyes and a confused yet lost look. Nora looked at her mom, and with a few back and forth, Kelly finally spoke up.

"I'm sorry, Miles. I saw the news, and I wanted to tell you that I hope they find your girlfriend," Kelly said.

Miles felt Nora's nervous energy. Miles knew it was bound to come up. Get it out of the way and close that chapter.

"Thak you. But I know Elana better than anyone. She is alright. Deep down I know that. I'm sure whatever she had going on, she just has to work through it," he paused and swallowed a choke. "She will be back."

Kelly was surprised by Miles's attitude. Miles watched as her questions washed away or at least were buried for the time bring. Nora winked at Miles, and he tried not to react. He still didn't want to give Kelly a wrong impression.

"What's taking so long? We're starving out here. Come on!" a male hollered from behind Miles.

Miles looked over his shoulder and saw one of Nora's brothers as he poked his head through the back door.

They look like twins.

"Hold your horses. I'll be there in a minute. Don't be rude and say hello to Miles," Kelly said. Nora brought a date."

"Hello, Miles," the brother said. He stepped backward and as he walked back out the back door, and announced, "Yo, Nora brought a date!"

Inside, Nora turned beet red

Nora patted Miles's shoulder, and he followed her toward the back.

"Let's just get this over with," Nora said.

Miles caught a glimpse at a picture as he walked outside. It was Nora, with her brothers, and father who were in their police uniforms.

"I'll be there in a few. Miles have a wonderful time," Kelly said.

Nora slid her hand into Miles's hand, gripped it tight and they headed out to the backyard. Right then, Miles saw their whole future. A white picketed fence, two point five kids, and a dog named Fluffy, chosen by the kids of course. This was what he wanted and would do anything to get it.

CHAPTER SEVENTEEN

CHECKERED TABLECLOTH

The backyard was like a dream. It reminded Miles of Heaven. He could spend days in the garden he made with his own two hands, name all the different flowers. Like the rooftop, Miles walked in each small aisle. He stopped and bent down to a row of blow and yellow daisies. Miles loved that they were vibrant, strong and in full bloom. Miles was speechless. And he thought he had a green thumb.

"I knew you were going to love it," Nora said.

"I do," Miles said.

In the middle, a long picnic table was set up with newspapers, which were being held down by table holders. Nora's brother, Chris, was tall and skinny as a rail and alluded to the latest basketball game by showing how he would have played in last night's game acting like the pitcher and batter.

Jacob, who is average height, muscular with high cheekbones, joked and laughed as one of their wives held a small child in jeans overalls with a baseball cap. Her dad, Thomas, stood in front of a large silver open boiler; when he opened it, smoke billowed into the air and the smell of deliciousness followed. A birthday sign hangs as balloons sway in the light breeze.

"I bet you never thought you would be here for a family barbeque," Nora said.

"No, but I'm glad I am. It wakes my mind off Elana and the search," Miles said.

Nora dug her foot into the topsoil. Miles knew she wanted to ask or say something.

"Go ahead," Miles said.

"Why aren't you there? At the trail I mean," Nora asked.

Miles searched for an answer but was saved by Alex, Nora's nephew.

"Aunt Nora!" Alex said.

Thank you, Alex.

Alex took a running start before leaping into her arms, and she caught him without any trouble. Miles thought he was adorable—blonde, small, and always smiling. Most of the kids resembled Nora and her brothers, so it was strange that Alex didn't look like them at all. Miles pondered what he and Nora's kids would look like if they had children.

"Alex. Oh, you're getting so big," Nora said as she bounced him to get some balance.

"Who's he?" Alex asked as he pointed at Miles.

"His name is Miles and he's my best friend," Nora said.

First, best friend, come on, Miles had been working toward something more than that. But Miles was happy to be called her best friend. It sounded much better when described as "friends with benefits." But he can't think about that, especially as Alex stared at him. Miles offered his hand to Alex. He also spoke in a silly, deep voice, which made Alex laugh.

Miles extended his hand, and Alex instantly hugged him. Miles glanced at Nora, who was all smiles. He never mentioned he doesn't like kids. Miles had never felt so uncomfortable in his entire life. Alex left and went back to play with his cousins. Nora looked shocked.

"Wow! He doesn't do that unless it's family. There must be something he sees. Like I do. Y'all this is Miles," Nora said as she walked backward.

I am in a house full of cops. But I'm with you, so...I'll just have to deal. Smile...

Time passed quickly. Splattered crawfish, corn, and potatoes all over old newspaper. The family dove in. Nora sat across from him and laughed with her brothers as they told stories about all the times she played cops and robbers with them. She was always the thief who got caught. Miles could see it in her playful demeanor.

Miles watched as Nora smiled at him while the children gathered around and bombarded him with questions like what his favorite color was.

Nora talked with her sister-in-law in the corner, and Miles realized she was discussing him by her stolen glances carefully averted, yet unable to resist stealing looks. He finds her breathtaking in the garden, her presence captivating.

Miles and Thomas walked through the garden as Mies explained flower care and their specific requirements, water needs, and potential improvements they could make to the garden. He offered to help fill the garden's gaps. Back inside the house, Miles listened as Marie spoke of how proud she was of her family by showing him family photographs, shared stories, and laugh at Nora's amusing expressions as she grew up.

While they carried some large silver platters, Nora paused and looked directly at Miles and blocked her oldest brother Jacob's path. Her gaze held a complexity of an unspoken understanding as she bobbed her head for Miles to follow her.

Miles couldn't pry his gaze away from her, even as Kelly playfully hit his chest, and laughed about the story she shared with him. As Nora walked away, she glanced back at him before she disappeared. Miles had to find out where she went. He excused himself and left Kelly alone.

Miles pushed open Nora's bedroom door, she twirled around and ended up sliding her knees into the cozy nook in front of her window. Her bed was a soothing blue, with a white feathery blanket draped elegantly over it; everything in the room is spotless, with not a speck of dust in sight. The dresser mirror is covered with an assortment of magazine cutouts featuring eyes, noses, mouths, and body parts of women and men, a testament to her creative and eclectic personality. Nora motioned for him to come closer, and as he peered out the window, he was met with the somber sight of a cemetery, a stark contrast to the warmth and vibrancy of her bedroom.

"The best view in the entire house," Nora said as she stared out the window. "Growing up I would sit and stare for hours. There's something serene about it."

Nora pointed towards the back of the cemetery to a small bench near the tree line.

"There was an old man who used to sit every day. Until one day, he was buried across from it," Nora said.

She cast a glance over her shoulder; her eyes locked onto his lips. Her gaze was intense, and her subtle, plump lips beckoned as she licked them, sending Miles's heart racing. The space between their lips was minimal, a mere few inches, for Miles the desire to kiss her, suck on her tongue, overwhelmed him. As Nora slowly rose to her feet, the air was electric. The attraction between them was palpable, stronger than anything Miles had ever experienced before. Miles knew both knew that they wanted to surrender to the passion that burned between them. As she lowered her chin, he raised his hand to meet it, his fingers curled gently.

"I don't think so," he whispered, his voice barely audible.

The connection between them was undeniable; they needed each other. With his fingers still curled, he lightly touched her cheek, and she closed her eyes, her breathing rapidly. He bent down, his lips inches from hers, ready to taste the sweetness of her mouth. Just as their lips were about to meet, her brother entered the room, shattering the intimate moment.

"Hey, y'all. It's cake time," Chris said.

Mile pushed himself away from Nora quickly. Nora sat in the nook as if she was looking out the window, and Miles moved over to her mirror, acting like he was checking out the picture glued to it.

"So, you cut all these out yourself?" Miles asked.

"Uh, yeah. Just a little project I used to do. You know collecting body – parts," Nora said.

"So, mom and dad want y'all to come down and – what were y'all doing?" Chris asked.

"Nothing. Just talking about, about pictures. No biggie," Nora answered.

"Really? Because it looked like you were about to make a move on a man whose girlfriend is missing," Chris reminded them.

"Didn't you say cake time?" Nora asked as she walked toward her bedroom door. She turned to me, "You coming, Miles?"

"Famished," Miles said.

Chris grabbed Miles's arm. Miles was nervous. Christ stared him down.

"Don't let her become everything in your life or forget who you are, and don't forget those in your life. She has a problem of becoming the main one in the relationship," Chris said.

What an odd thing to say.

"Thanks for the warning," Miles said.

Thank you, Mom, for not having any more mes I would kill them.

***

Marie walked out with a large cake with a candle already burning. She sang "Happy Birthday" to Kelly. Miles sat there confused. When he glanced around and everyone seemed sad, which is far from how you're supposed to be at a birthday party.

"Who's Kelly?" Miles whispered to Nora.

Miles looked into Nora's eyes as she searched for an answer. But Miles never got one when Nora and he snapped their eyes to a problem that entered the yard.

"Did someone forget to invite me?" a male's voice interrupted.

Before anyone could respond, Paul Dobson, a tall, rough, drunken, and half-dressed New Orleans police officer in uniform, walked through the back gate. Nora's brothers slowly stood up, their wives gathered the kids and headed inside, and Kelly dropped the cake on the table in shock.

The atmosphere was tense as Nora locked onto Paul. Nora's gaze radiated anger.

It was clear Paul's presence was unwelcome, especially in his drunken state, which added to the sense of unease that settled over the gathering. As Nora's eyes narrowed, her rage and disgust were palpable, leaving onlookers to wonder who this man was and what his connection was to Nora. The question on Miles's mind was what he wanted.

"Why'd you stop? Come on. Sing with me. Happy birthday to you, happy birthday to you. Dear Marie. Happy birthday to you," Paul sang.

Paul flailed his arms and urged everyone to join as Thomas rushed at him with Chris and Jacob close behind. Miles could tell they were ready for a fight; their body language radiated it. Chris cracked his knuckles inside his palm, while Jacob scowled and narrowed his eyes as he watched Paul's every move with an unblinking gaze. Meanwhile, a sense of unease settles in, prompting a strong instinct to be near Nora. Getting up and walking over to her, a protective stance is taken. Nora, it's clear she doesn't need or want protection, but it's offered.

Thomas snapped, "You're not welcome here, Paul."

Paul reacted like a child and rolled his eyes, and responded with, "Come on, Thomas. This is about family. And I'm part of it."

Chris strongly interjected, his teeth clenched, "He said you're not welcome."

Paul shifted his gaze back and forth between the men in front of him. Eventually, he settled on Nora. A sly grin spread across his face, reminiscent of the Big Bad Wolf who sized up a little pig, right before he attacked. Miles stepped in front of Nora to shield her from Paul. The atmosphere is charged with anticipation, as if the situation could escalate at any moment, and Miles couldn't wait.

"You're looking more and more like her every day, Nora. How about we take a little walk?"

I dare you motherfucker.

"Fuck you, Paul," Nora yells, surrounds me.

"I get it. I get it. I like you, Nora. I like you a lot," Paul roars, laughing.

I want you to take a step forward. It's amazing what I can do with a plastic fork and knife. Come on, Paul. Want to find out? I dare you to tempt me.

"Go home, Paul. Before…" Thomas said.

"Before what? Before you call the cops?" Paul said with a spit laugh.

Paul stretched out his arms and circled them around a few times.

"Sorry, Captain. I think I'm – we're already here," Paul said.

Thomas got nose to nose with Paul. Both had their chests out; Jacob placed his hand on Chris's shoulder as Thomas stepped beside him. Paul smirked.

"I've always hated this place," Paul said.

Paul spat at Thomas's feet. Chris jumped at Paul, who laughed his head off. He shook his fingers like he was scared, then pulled out another cigarette as Thomas and Jacob tried to get Chris's attention. I pulled Nora's arms around my waist, and he breathed on my arm. It was hot and heavy. Suddenly, Alex comes running down the stairs, jumps the stairs, and is happy to see Paul.

"Daddy!" Alex shouted, excitedly.

Before anyone could stop him, Alex jumped into Paul's arms.

"Hey, buddy," Paul said as he picked Alex up.

"Daddy. I miss you," Alex said.

Paul wrapped his arms around Alex and held him tight as everyone stared, and waited for him to do something.

"I miss you so much too," Paul said.

"When can I come home?" Alex asked.

"Just a little bit longer. Daddy has a few things to tie up. But you'll be home soon," Paul said.

"Yay!" Alex exclaimed as he wrapped his arms around Paul's neck in a hug.

The awkwardness, fear, and hatred – flowed through the air. Miles didn't need a knife to cut it, all he had to do was slice my hand through it. Alex slid down and Paul bent down to meet his level.

"Be good for you Grandma. Now, go get some cake and wish mommy a happy birthday. She would love it hear it," Paul said as he straightened up.

"Ok. I love you, daddy," Alex said as he crawled onto the bench.

"I love you too, son," Paul leered at Thomas, "He's my son not yours. Best remember that when court rolls around," he glances p like to the heavens and said, "Happy fucking birthday bitch,"

"Time for you to," Thomas said.

Paul turned to leave when he hesitated and pointed at Nora.

"I'll see you real soon," Paul said to Nora with a wink. winking.

There won't be a next time by the time I get done with you. I'm thinking bottle down the throat will be the funniest and worse way to die for you, Paul. Maybe even two the way I'm feeling.

Nora walked away. Jacob paced as he waited for Paul to show back up, and Chris moved hugged at back down with his wife at the picnic table. Miles was confused.

"Who was that?" Miles asked.

"Paul Dobson. Dirty ass cop, drunk, ex-brother-in-law, and the guy who murdered my sister. Kelly," Chris replied.

Holy shit! And here I thought my family was fucked up. Nora, what have you been hiding from me?

CHAPTER EIGHTEEN

LONG DRIVE HOME

Nora remained silent as they made their way to Miles's car. Miles had never seen her so terrified, angry, and baffled since we met. She refused to speak. Miles knew she would tell him everything when she was ready. All Miles had was time. Time, as far as Paul knew, was not going to be on his side if he touched her. He would deliver his head to you on a silver platter for Nora if that happened.

"Do you want me to drive you home?" Miles asked.

"No. I think I'll stay here for a little longer and then call a cab," Nora said.

"Nora, I -" Miles said.

But Nora had a different plan for Miles, and when it happened, he wasn't ready for the rage.

"What the fuck was that?" Nora asked.

Confused, Miles stood there with a dumb look on his face. He searched his mind for something but came up blank. He opened his mouth to talk but was cut off.

"You didn't have to step in front of me like that. I can take care of myself," Nora said.

"I know. I was just..." Miles said.

"I am stronger, faster, and a whole of hell lot smarter than Paul, and you. So, don't try to placate me into thinking I need a hero. I'm the villain in this story, and I fucking like it," Nora said.

Miles was shocked when Nora shoved him. It was hard.

"Whoa, what is happening? I can't tell if you're joking or," Miles said when she shoved him again.

She shoved him again. And this time she didn't back down. All Miles could do was try and stay on his feet for balance. He couldn't believe Nora pushed him all the way to the passenger's side door, which he hit the car with a thud after he missed the curve.

He watched as she stopped. She just stared at him. It took her a minute before she came back down to earth from rage city. Miles watched as the darkness in her eyes faded and her hazel eyes came back into view.

She parted her lips to speak, instead she just left. Each stomp she took back to her parent's house was short, fast, and came with a thunderous rage. When she turned back to Miles, she glared at him with so much disdain and hatred, Miles broke a little inside. He thought he was angry. Her expression was fierce and knotted.

"Where are you going?" Miles asked.

"Goodnight," Nora yelled as she slammed the door.

And there goes the porch light. In every movie Miles has seen, the girl always turns off the light. Like it's supposed to scare people or a sense if rejection. It's worse than rejection.

CHAPTER NINETEEN

WHEEL OF FORTUNE AND STORMS

It had been a few days since Miles spoke with Nora. After the fourth call went to voicemail, he felt he had blown it. And he had no idea what that was. He did not want to bother her or witness her fury again. It reminded him of so much, and he understood it. He wanted to learn more about it. He was concerned about her safety right now, not because of Paul, but because of the impending hurricane heading into New Orleans.

Miles closed early. He was going through the business making sure everything was locked, but how much can one building do when a hurricane hits? He gathered as many flowers as possible and arranged them in the back. While he did, he wondered what Heathcliff would do if the hurricane destroyed Petal Perfection. Would he still want the land? Miles didn't want to find out. He turned off the lights near the front door, started to walk toward the back, when he stopped. There was a rapid knock on the door.

Who the hell would be out in this?

Again, whoever it was knocked again.

"Yeah, yeah, I'm coming," Miles said.

Whoever it continued to knock, and it got on Miles nerves. He unlocked the door. He flung it open. It was Nora.

"Nora!" Miles said shocked.

Nora held up a sack full of Chinese food, and said, "I owe you an apology."

Accepted. Now, strip. We can eat Chinese after we fuck long, hard, and all night. Best way to ride out the impending hurricane – I'm down.

Nora stepped inside, her boot heels clicking on the floor. Miles had left the door open. She looked good in the natural light as she glanced around the semi-empty store except for some larger and heavier vases.

"Where are all the flowers?" Nora asked as she twirled around, and the food balanced her out.

"They are in the back. Safe and sound, at least I hope so.," Miles said. He stood on his tiptoes and tried to see what was in the bag. "That's a lot of food for an apology."

Nora held it out in front of her and said, "I didn't know what you wanted or liked, so I got one of everything. Well, *almost* everything." She lowered her arm with the food. "I really am sorry."

"No, don't worry about it," Miles said. "I shouldn't have jumped up and in the way I did."

"You didn't deserve it. Especially my little rant," Nora said.

"Little rant? I think I might have a bruise after all that poking," Miles said as he rose and moved his shoulder in a circle.

"Ok, ok – I get it," Nora said.

"You are stronger than you look. If I need a bodyguard, can I hire you?" Miles said.

"Very funny. And I would protect you for free," Nora said.

And then there awas silence. The wind picked up and blew her hair from her face.

"I figured we could ride out the storm together," Nora said.

One problem. I'm not by myself.

"I will, but..." Miles said.

The loud sound came down the stairs from the apartment above. If Miles didn't know what it was, he might have thought it was the waves of the hurricane that were collapsing down upon him. but it was worse. Davis hurling down the stairs.

"Hey, Nora," Davis said.

Miles saw Nora's stunned look. Miles never mention him and the woman in tow behind him, Renee, his girlfriend, who had been living in the apartment for a couple of months now. Renee waved at Nora with so much excitement; she pushed past Davis and headed straight toward Nora.

"Davis, I didn't know you were here," Nora said. "And?"

Renee hugged Nora, and said, "I'm Renee. Davis's girlfriend."

"Yeah, she's my main squeeze," Davis said.

Renee pulled back and said, "I'm his lemon to his lime."

I didn't have a chance to say anything. Well, I did in that awkward, sensual (sensual what, I should have grabbed you and kissed you. But that didn't happen.

"I have the best boss – oooh, it that what I think it is. I could smell it all the way upstairs," Davis said.

Davis breathed in the delicious sweet and sour aromas from the bag. Instantly, he took it to the counter and began to pull out the containers. Nora chuckled.

"I have an idea to pass the time. If y'all are up for it," Nora suggested as she tapped the camera hanging around her neck.

The thunder rumbled and the lights flickered. She eased her neck up and watched it. It never went out. But Miles had a feeling it would.

"With the storm, I think this might be a bad time.," Miles said.

But I don't want you to leave. You're safe with me. If I want this so bad, then why am I always stopping myself with these lame ass excuses. Buck up, Miles and have a little fucking fun. Shit...

"I think it's a perfect time," Nora said as she walked past him.

***

Her smile gets me every time.

With each click of the camera, Nora bent down and to the side of Renee. She moved to Davis, took the bundle of wildflowers from him and handed them to Miles.

"Stay still," Nora said.

I will do whatever you want. Just don't stop. Nora can do anything she wants me to.

Miles stuck out his tongue. Nora laughed. Renee walked from behind the desk, and she shook a case full of plastic vases. One by one, the vases are set up. The plastic bottles are arranged to resemble the shape of bowling pins. Each of them took turns with a large green foam ball. Davis completely missed the vase. Miles knocked them all down and then walked over to Nora, which made her smirk. With a foam ball in hand, Nora aims and knocks them all down. She strutted and then laughed. Challenge accepted. Renee cheered as she knocked down one and ran into Davis's arms. They kiss. Nora and Miles looked at each other.

Davis comes rushing out the back with a disco ball. He holds it up with a goofy smile. Renee gets giddy. Where did he find that? Miles shook his head and looked at Nora, who smiled and said, "Put it up." Miles sighed. He felt like he was in hell. But the smile on Nora's face made it a little less hot.

Davis and Renee begin posing for photos while Nora continuously snapped pictures of them. Davis lay on the stool like he was swimming, and Renee posed like a 1920s pin-up girl.

Nora said, "Perfect. Give me something else."

Miles limply turns the disco ball again.

Miles stood in the middle with a rose between his teeth.

"I love it," Nora said.

Miles made the Hulk's arms flex. Renee posed in so many ways as Davis pointed a fan toward her. Her hair flew everywhere. Davis popped his collar up and gave Nora the potty lips look, which was popular on social media. Miles thought he looked like a fish.

Renee passed flowers to Davis, who gently took them and cradled them in his arms. Nora stepped closer to Miles. She thanked Renee, while Miles felt like an idiot with a flower crown. Nora snaps pictures quickly, seemingly capturing every moment before Miles can take it off. She rushes up and tries to put the crown back on, but Miles playfully places it on her head instead.

As Nora stood there changing the camera's film, she looked at Miles with what he called "dreamy eyes" wholesome and innocent. But Miles knew she was not as innocent as she appeared to be. He found himself curious about her hidden wicked ways.

Shutting the camera's back, Davis walked up. Somehow, Nora has handed him her camera. He shooed her into the background. Miles moved out of the way, Renee took the stool, and Davis shoved Nora and took center stage.

She appeared visibly uncomfortable, and Miles noticed she was not accustomed to being a model. She seemed tense from head to toe. Miles walked over and shook her shoulders from behind to help her loosen up. He noticed she was uncharacteristically shy, a side of her he had yet to see until now. Everyone has their vulnerabilities, and Miles saw Nora's and fell harder for her.

As Miles began to walk away, Nora pulled him back. If she had to have her picture taken, so did Miles. Miles didn't need to be persuaded.

Miles held her close. Davis snapped the picture as Renee stood on the step stool and tossed red, white, and pink petals above them. Miles loved the idea of raining flowers. Nora tried to walk away, but was pulled her back by the end of her jacket.

I'm never going to give you up, Nora. You might as well get used to it.

As Miles dipped her, he imagined it was just Nora and himself there. She gradually began to rise. Miles saw every muscle and vein in her neck stretch, and she could see her pulse bulge under her skin. Miles knew she was excited and was ready for his touch. All Miles wanted to do was taste her. The shop floor became a bed of roses as Miles lowered her carefully, with red, white, and yellow petals floating in the air as they landed. Miles kissed her neck. Miles knew by her reaction and gentle moans. She liked his tongue on her by the way she arched her back.

Miles ran his hand down the center of her chest. She wasn't wearing a bra which turned Miles on. Miles unbuttoned her shirt. He placed his hand over her right breast. He noticed it was very firm. He was pretty sure Nora had barely anybody fat. She rubbed up against his body as she raised her leg. He raised her hands above her head, pinned them with my right hand, and creeped his other hand between her legs. A camera flashed all around them.

"*I want you so bad,*" *Miles whispered*

"*Then take me,*" *Nora said.*

She moaned as Miles slipped inside her. His grip on her hands above her grew tighter with every thrust. Deeper, he descended as rose petals continued to fall on top of them.

I have a sickness. Nora is my cure.

Suddenly, everything went dark. And Miles's daydream ended.

"Light went out," Davis said.

CHAPTER TWENTY

GONE DARK

On the same bar stool that they used in the photoshoot sat a square black radio. Miles turned up the volume and listened to the weather report and slid over to the circle lit up with a few lanterns he found deep inside the storage room. Nora ate one of the eggs rolls she had brought.

"Looks like the hurricane has been downgraded to a tropical storm. Better than last year but still stay indoors until further notice. Until then, enjoy the song 'Stay with Me' by Sam Smith," the DJ said.

Miles settled down and picked up a white food box and chopsticks. Across from him were Davis and Renee, who were sound asleep. He heard little snores coming from Davis and a whistle sound from Renee. Outside, the wind blew, and rain poured which made it sound like bells being hit the window. Nora stared at David and Renee.

"Isn't funny how they can sleep through this?" Nora said.

"Ah, they're used to it. We all are," Miles said as he took a big bite of soy sauce-soaked noodles.

Nora dug into her General Tso's chicken and glanced up at Davis as he pulled Renee tighter into him. Miles could tell she was thinking about something.

Share it with me. I want to hear everything you're thinking about.

"Spill," Miles said,

"I don't want to upset you," Nora said as she stabbed at her chicken.

Nothing you could possibly say is stupid.

"No, really tell me. It will pass the time," Miles said as he motioned to the storm outside.

"Why does he want your shop so bad?" Nora asked.

Miles knew it was about Heathcliff. She was here when we came the other week. So, it was just a matter of time before she asked. Miles wondered if she already knew since she had access to a few things. He wondered what she would say if he told her that Heathcliff broke some laws. But Miles has a plan of his own to solve the Heathcliff problem.

"It's not really the flower shop he wants. It's the land, or rather the waterway behind it," Miles said.

"Wait. He wants the lake?" Nora asked. "How can he?"

"You know how schools redistrict every few years?" Miles asked.

"No, but go on," Nora said.

"Well, a few years ago New Orlean redistricted the waterway," Miles said. "And it so happens the majority of the waterway is connected to my small property the flower shop sits on," Miles said.

"And that goes for the rest of the street," Nora said.

"Bingo," Miles said.

Miles picked up a bottle of water and drank it as Nora kept going.

"So, you own the waterway. Holy shit, you must be making bank," Nora said.

"Wrong. I don't own anything accept the shop, and what little land it's on. It's not like I have oil on my land," Miles said.

Except for the garden in the lake in the back.

"The board who decides the new lines, can change it anytime they want," Miles said.

"Then make them change it," Nora said.

"Guess who's on the board," Miles said.

"Heathcliff Morand," Nora said. "Damn."

The storm was about to hit land as the lightning struck in the dark sky, thunder rolled in, and the wind picked up.

"Let's say you sell. I know you're not. But if you did, what would happen to Davis?" Nora asked.

"I don't know. I would try my best to find him work. He means too much to me. I refuse to see him like he was," Miles said.

Nora stayed silent.

"Three years ago. Davis was homeless and I caught him digging the trash cans in the back one day. He saw me and ran. I couldn't help myself. I would go and buy the stores out of food, then hide them in the trash cans, and wait. He came back every day. Then one day I offered him a job, and he's been here ever since. Honestly, I don't know what I would do without him. He's like a brother to me," Miles said.

Maybe I really can tell you anything...everything.

"That's amazing, Miles. Most people would have had him arrested or worse," Nora says, soft and quiet.

I see your sensitive side, and I'm completely attracted to it. More than I already am. If that's possible.

"I'm not most people." Miles said.

"That is true Miles Pike. You are one of a kind," Nora said.

"You have no idea," Miles said.

"You someone should teach Heathcliff Morand a lesson," Nora said.

"I couldn't agree more," Miles said.

Nora grabbed two fortune cookies and handed one to Miles. He watched as she used her teeth to rip it open. She cracked open the cookie and pulled out a small oblong piece of paper. As he watched, Nora's expression shifted from excitement to bewilderment and confusion.

"What is it?" Miles asked.

Nora turned the paper, and Miles saw that it was completely blank. It was the first time Miles had ever witnessed a fortuneless fortune cookie.

"I guess there's nothing in my fortune. I better make the best of it while I'm still here," Nora said.

Miles plucked the paper from her fingertips and got up and walked over to the front desk. Miles wrote down her fortune—the fortune she deserved—then tossed the pen down and flashed her a smile. He sat back down and handed it to her.

"*'Happiness is just a click away.*' Love the camera pun. and you even drew a little camera," Nora said.

"Sebastian Faena, Cass Bird, or Paul Bellaart, I'm not. But it fits," Miles said.

"Someone has been Googling well-known photographers. I'm impressed," Nora said.

"Well, maybe a little," Miles said as he looked around.

Nota chuckled. The moment between them was small, but Miles knew that look. She felt something for him right then and there. She punched his arm to break the silence.

"So, here I am locked in a flower shop during an impending hurricane with a devilishly handsome man and a camera," Nora said, sarcastically and batted her eyes.

"Flattery will get you everywhere." Miles said.

For someone who acts happy. She doesn't seem like it.

"Are you happy, Nora?" Miles asked.

"Yeah, yeah – I am. I have a great family. I have a good career whether I become a famous photographer whose pictures in *Vogue*. And I have amazing friends. One being you, of course," Nora said.

Fuck friend zones. Let's cross it and be something more. In every way possible. Whoever comes up with friend zones needs to be dragged across the street and shot.

"What about you?" Nora asked.

"I'm happy. I have friends, this place, you, and my garden of girls," Miles said.

"Any family?" Nora asked.

Family? I don't even know where to start, Nora. It's very complicated.

"My dad left when I was ten. My mother raised me. She taught me everything I know about flowers. It was her passion. Now it's mine," Miles said.

Forget the fact I strangled her to death. Not because I wanted to. But because she asked me. I'll tell you more about her when we get closer. I promise. Also, about the rules. So many of them.

"She must be proud of you," Nora said,

"I think she is," Miles said.

"Oh, I thought she was – I didn't mean," Nora said.

"No, no. no. She's not dead. She's in a nursing home. She lost it after my dad left. Depression, anxiety, so many things made her sink deep inside the darkness that became her life. I talk to her and seer as much as I can," Miles said.

You might look at me differently if I blatantly say I see and have conversations with my dead mother. You could even run away from me. I never want that. I want you to see the real me. Caring, nurturing even. But not a killer.

"Well, she raised an amazing man," Nora said.

Nora cradled her arms and rubbed them up and down. Miles got the drape the sheet she used as a backdrop and placed it over her shoulders. She cinched it around her waist and pulled it tight around her.

"Amazing and considerate. What are the odds?"

Another awkward moment descended upon them. He thought he should say something interesting but drew a blank. Thankfully, Davis's loud snore unexpectedly shattered the uncomfortable atmosphere. Nora put her head in Miles's lap. He wanted more, deeper, meaningful. It was easier said than done.

"I've never met anyone like you, Miles Pike," Nora said quietly.

"I was going to say the same thing about you, Nora Asher," Miles said.

"You asked me if I was happy," Nora said. "I wasn't until I met you."

Miles felt unsafe and exposed. She turned her head from him. Miles felt like every brick he had ever built around himself was breaking down and left him defenseless. He thought he was ready.

"Elana is so lucky," Nora said.

"Nora, I have to tell you something. Something about me, " Miles said.

"What is it?" Nora said as she yawned.

"It's – I'm - I'm not who you think... I've done things. Horrible things, I don't know how to say this. But I've ki... Nora? "

A smile crossed Miles's face when he saw Nora was asleep in his lap. While starting to stroke her hair, he knew what he had to do and what he wanted to do. He trusted her. He loved her.

He had all these rules, but when he was with her, none of them seemed to matter, and he couldn't figure out why. He leaned back against the wall, and listened to the rain. He would tell her another day. Until then, he was just quiet and enjoyed the moment. When she's ready, Miles would tell her about Elana, and his other flowers.

CHAPTER TWENTY-ONE

GOLDEN GORILLA HIT

Miles stared in disbelief; his mind reeled with shock and betrayal. Was this really supposed to be a paradise for lovers? Miles let the flowers fall to his side, feeling mocked and betrayed by his relationship. He couldn't believe Elana could do this to him, especially after everything he had done for her. He had been nothing but loyal, the best partner anyone could ask for, and here she was barely clothed. He had never even seen that outfit.

His thoughts spiraled, questioning the situation and his own perceptions. Why couldn't he make sense of what was happening? Elana stood there and tried to look innocent, but Miles assumed she was calculating her next move. Or at least, a good explanation.

A mixture of hurt and rage started to burn inside Miles. He had so many questions, but only one would come out. And it wasn't the one he wanted.

"How was the trail?" Miles asked.

"I can explain all of this," Elana said. "I'm visiting my cousin."

"Come on, you can do better than that," Miles said.

Over his shoulder, mayo man chuckles. as he takes another bite of his sandwich. Hey pal!

I hope you choke.

"It's not what you think?" Elana said.

How many times is she going to say that? Too little, too late Elana.

"Really? Then what is it?" Miles asked.

Miles pushed past Elana said, "Put some clothes on."

She rolled her eyes and let out a sigh of exasperation, clearly unbothered by his remark as Miles tossed the flowers onto the kitchen island.

"Really, Miles?" she said with a hint of amusement in her voice, "I thought you were here to deliver flowers, not critique my wardrobe."

Miles glanced around. He wasn't impressed with what he saw. There's not one drop of her personality here. He personally loves the simple table, not the lemon sculpture with an eye that stared at him for the living room. Miles thought it was creepy. The area rug covered much of the open space between the front door and the dark blue couch with white pillows with embroidered crawfish on them. A blue chair with a long orange carrot sitting in it.

"I know I should have told you. But I didn't know how to bring it up," Elana said.

"You didn't know how to bring it up. Well," Miles said as he slapped his hand on his legs. "Well, now would be a good time."

There's never going to be a good time for what she's about to tell me. I just know it.

As he walked away from her, a headache crawled up the back of his head like a spider.

"I was – you were working late one night when we were supposed to go to dinner, and I went. I was sitting alone, then this guy came up and asked if I was ok. And talked and the next thing I know we started dating," Elana said. "It just happened."

Miles didn't know what to say.

What just happened?

"It just happened," Miles said.

Elana crossed her arms and said, "Yeah, it did."

Miles laughed and repeated, "It just happened."

He saw Elana confused and stunned. He kept repeating, it just happened, when his laugh turned into a yell. Miles grabbed the roses off the kitchen island and destroyed them with every yank and pull of the petals. Miles heard himself yell but he didn't know how loud he was. He walked quickly toward Elana, who dropped her arms to her side.

"How could you do this to me?" Miles said. "I love you so much."

"It was an accident," Elana says with a smile.

"An accident? I work late and you accidentally fall on some other guy's dick," Miles said.

"I fell on a lot of them," Elana said as she laughed at him.

Miles couldn't stand it when someone laughed at him, especially his girlfriend. She walked back up to him as if she were challenging him. He stared at her and saw something in her eyes he had never seen. Between all the movie nights, dinners, amusement park rides when the fair was in, and the shows at the art gallery Mr. Stansbury had that they went to, and all the game nights with her friends. The light and love she had in her eyes for Miles, was gone. It was replaced with a whore.

"Do you want the truth?" Elana asked. "I have been so bored with you."

Elana stepped closer to Miles. He felt her slender, pedicured fingers as she walked them up his chest. Miles looked down at her fingers and then backed up from Elana.

"I was with you for my daddy. He thought you were the perfect man. You own a business, cared what he thought and more than anything was utterly devoted to me. All I cared about was making him happy. See if I didn't curve my wild ways, then I would be cut off. You made look responsible by doing everything. And I got to do whatever I wanted. It's not you're going to leave me. I'm the best you will ever do, Miles," Elana said.

She flicked his forehead.

"Get fucked," Miles said.

"I plan on it," Elana said. She walked away and pointed at the door. "Get the fuck out."

Bad choice of words, Elana. If there's one thing my mother taught me, it's to never let someone disrespect you. Never let anyone talk down to you. Never be someone you're not. And never, ever let someone break one of your rules. And if they do, Punish them.

Miles was numb. He felt like he was walking outside of his body as he picked up the golden gorilla statue that sat on the end table. He heard Elana as she talked to him.

"What are you waiting for? Want a goodbye fuck or something? I don't have time to fake it again," Elana said.

"Elana," Miles said.

He stared off not space and remembered what had happened.

As Elana turned around, Miles swung.

Miles hit Elana square in the face as hard as he could. She fell to the floor with a thud. She had already begun to struggle for air. The hit had collapsed her nose into her face, broken her jaw, and blinded her with blood. Miles turned to see her as she moved around on the floor but was able to get up. Miles stepped over and straddled her. She spit out blood, and Miles stared down. He wanted her to see what was coming her way. He bent down and wiped the blood from and around her eyes. She opened them. Miles wondered if she could see him. If not, then she would see the gorilla head her way again.

"I have a set the rules, and when they are broken, I have to fix them," Miles said.

Elana tried to move but Miles sat on her stomach and locked his knees onto her sides. She wasn't going anywhere. He lifted the gorilla. Elana started to cry.

"Shhhhh. There, there, little girl. Let me dry your tears," Miles said.

Miles bought down the gorilla repeatedly. The gold was painted crimson as Elana screamed. With each hit, her scream faded. Miles were decorated in her blood. He licked his lips, then smiled as her blood coated his teeth. Three. Ten, Seventeen. Twenty-three. Miles didn't know when Elana stopped her screams, not her breathing, All Miles knew was that she needed to learn her lesson: never look a gift horse in the mouth.

"See, missionary isn't so bad," Miles said.

Silence. Elana went limp as her body flattened and threaded itself into the rug beneath her.

Don't worry, Nora, I'm confessing all my sins in my special way to you, and I hope you're listening in a non-judgmental way, unlike Elana. She always has. Why are you doing it this way? How about you do it that way? My daddy would have done, did, always with the daddy shit. Seriously, you would have thought she had mommy issues—not daddy ones. It's weird, Nora.

Miles bent down and played with her hair. He ran his fingers through it; she had great hair.

"I got off. Did you?" Miles asked.

CHAPTER TWENTY-TWO

HUSH NOW, LITTLE BUGABOO

The air seemed to be sucked out of the room, the second Miles realized Elana was dead. He bent closer to her and saw her bloody, unclean, glassy eyes. He wasn't going to close them as he typically would. Elana was different, she had always been different. A part of him hoped she might sense something, though he knew deep down this was merely wishful thinking.

Her skin remained warm to the touch as he traced a gentle circle in the middle of her palm. There was a strange sense of liberation now—the ability to say, think, and be exactly what he wanted without Elana. Maybe even find someone who loved him for him.

"Fucking bitch."

Miles slapped Elana across the face. It was a wet slap. He hit her hard enough that her head was cocked to the side as if she looked at the balcony.

Okay, think Miles. Normally, I would have these planned out. Oh well, everything happens for a reason, Nora. And now you are my reason.

"I bet you're wondering what happened to the guy you were seeing. Let's just say his wife wasn't too happy to get a bouquet of flowers for you from him. Did I mention she read the card at her baby shower," Miles said.

First thing first, Miles had to place Elana somewhere. Hidden for now. It is too small. big enough for jackets but not a body. Leaning against the closet door, Miles scanned the kitchen. The cabinets are too small. Miles started to freak out. He could think of anything to do with her.

Miles rushed around the place and searched for Elana's things. He went into the bedroom where he found her suitcase in the corner. After he picked it up, it opened, and some of the things fell out. He gathered blue, pink, black, and green thongs, which she never wore for him, and tossed them back inside the suitcase as he went through the rest of the room.

From the closet, he grabbed her fresh, ironed jeans, shirts, and some boots, and placed them. He rushed inside the bathroom, where he grabbed her makeup bag and threw it into the trash can. He pulled back the shower curtain and grabbed her body wash, shampoo, and conditioner.

Miles remembered he saw a trunk in the corner of the living room. It was perfect. Miles opened it and found it was empty.

Elana, my love, I found you a place to stay for the time being. Maybe you will think about what you did. Miles picked up Elana and stuffed her inside the trunk. It wasn't like Elana was going to say something. Miles pushed so hard, he heard a crack as he folded her inside the chest. He locked it. Miles stood and thought for a minute. He headed into the kitchen, to clean up.

Tine dwindled fast. Elana's phone stared at him from the coffee table. Miles didn't know if it was going to work, but he had to try. Miles sat down on the couch and clicked her phone on. He was shocked that she had a passcode. Obviously, she didn't trust people. She didn't trust him. Mile was taught cheaters always had one.

OK, think. Important dates No, not the day we met. My birthday, nope. Her birthday, nope. Damnit. Then it hit me like a ton of bricks. No, she couldn't have his name as her passcode. C-H-E-T. Unlock. Fuck, she was with Chet.

Miles searched through Elana's photos and picked one that was recent. She was smiling while she posed like a body builder on the side of a mountain. That was when he noticed the woman in the picture wasn't her. It was a stock photo from an internet site. She had changed a few things but at a distance it looked like her. He opened Instagram. It's from a few years ago when she was on vacation in Colorado. It's captioned: I'm happy to be here. Time to get my photo on. Later, y'all.

"You have been a busy girl with all these dating apps, Elana. How many times have you cheated on me? No wonder you always have a cold."

More like an STD. Lucky me I never got anything except a cheating, good for nothing bitch who deserved everything she got.

He kicked the chest. He wanted to kill her all over again. Wanted to drag her out and smother her all over again. The fact he knew Elana had stock photos made him think she was never where she said she was. He wondered how long she had been here. Miles decided it was the perfect time for Elana to go on a little self-discovery trip.

Miles opened Instagram and wrote, Hey, y'all. Got an opp of a lifetime and it's so going to be my new venture. Art is out. Self-discovery is in. Bringing a few things with me. Lemonhead, a small overnight bag, and of course y'all. Post in a week or two. Gotta learn the ropes to be able to climb. Duh, you know what I mean. Love ya, Elana!

Miles posted it and then copy and pasted the same thing onto all her social media along with all her dating apps she's on. The post wasn't even five minutes as Miles watched men came out of the woodwork.

Nice to see you.

I was wondering where you were.

Miles smirked. Now to keep Elana alive.

Miles had to cover his tracks. He brought the flowers he destroyed back to the flower shop and tossed them in the dumpster in the back of the store.

He pulled out his phone and downloaded a texting app he could use to send to himself and others in the name of Elana. Elana's phone continued to ding so much that it became annoying so Miles checked it. Messages from a man named Bae. Miles knew who it was, the man who ordered the flowers who works for Heathcliff.

Did Heathcliff know Elana was sleeping with one of his employees? He must have. And if he did or did, then he would use it against Miles to get the shop. Another ding.

I might as well answer back. So, he did and said, "I'm sorry, babe. I need to find myself. I have so much happening in my life that I have to breathe and I can't when I am here. I have to hit the trails."

"What have I become?" Miles asked.

"I love this side of you," a female voice said.

Daydreaming took over a Miles turned his head to see Nora sitting on a stool on the kitchen island. He was imagining her because he wanted her to be there and share this moment with him. She was playing with one of the flower petals which was on the counter.

"Really," Miles said.

"I love everything about you," Nora said.

Nora got up. She never took her eyes off him as she walked toward him. She stepped over Elana's body and stood in front of him.

"Elana didn't know what she had. She didn't respect you or the relationship. She deserved everything you gave her," Nora said.

"I tried so hard. I thought she was the one," Miles said.

"She has never been the one, Miles," Nora said.

Nora slid her hand up my jeans and tugged Miles's zipper. Miles moved his arm in the air hoping to find something to hold on to as he listened to each click of my zipper unhook. Nora got down on her knees and buried her head in his crotch. She teased him with a few flicks of her tongue and turned her face at me. She wets her lips.

"Let me make you happy. I want you to make you happy. I will make," Nora said.

Miles never wanted it to end. He felt Nora's mouth all over him.

"Shit!" Miles said.

Miles continued to jerk off as he looked down and saw Nora wasn't there. It was just him and Elana. Her smashed face stared up at him with sperm all over it. Miles zipped up.

Before he opened the door, Miles glanced around one last time before he left. He was sure he got everything and left nothing to be found. He covered his tracks when it came to social media. Sent and answer texts to those who are in her life, which included himself. Basic and clean messages, and in her tone of voice. It wasn't the first time Elana disappeared for days or even weeks at a time. He knew he would have to extend the lie once it hit months if everything followed the plan he was still forming.

If not, he was fucked.

CHAPTER TWENTY-THREE

PLANTING ELANA

By the time Miles got to the lakefront, it was dark. He liked it that way because the fear of being seen wasn't there. If anyone did it was normal because Miles was always there, which was always part of his plan so no one would question him on a late-night row. He opened the trunk of his car and struggled to pull out the trunk with Elana in it. He pulled on part out and then carefully let the other side down.

You deserve a lot more than I am doing to you. I'm not mad. I'm fine. Really, I forgive for all the horrible things you said earlier. But I have to do what I have been for years, Punishment doesn't mean I don't love you. You're going to be one of my gorgeous floating flowers, Elana.

He dragged the chest down the wooden dock and listened as the water rippled and called his name. It called Elana's name as well. He unlocked the chest. Elana was there bent like an accordion.

"I love you," Miles said.

The chill off the top of the water sent shivers down Miles's spine. He loved that feeling. He had been there so many times he lost count until he saw them. Then he remembered how much they meant to him. His garden of girls.

Each time his oars plunged in and out of the water, all he could do was smile. They say people have their happy place. Well, this one was his.

I'm okay with sharing this with you, Nora. You need to know what and where I take care of them.

Elana laid half in and out of the small rowboat. Miles looked at her, and she was so peaceful, like Sleeping Beauty, and Miles was her Prince. But his kiss was deadly.

The anchor was as heavy as it looked. Miles imagined as the anchored descended, his flowers woke up from their withered state, looked up, and waited to see who was next. They had no fear because they loved Miles. Miles loved them more than anyone could ever know.

Nora, you have to understand that I am normal. As ordinary as they come. But a demon inside me takes over, and I have to feed it by making those who break my rules pay. I know, I know, it sounds stupid. But you will understand.

He lifted Elana like a ragdoll. Mile's mother once told him that if he didn't teach them how to be, then he would end up like his father. Miles couldn't let that happen. Miles grinned as Elana disappeared into the ark water. Miles knew Elana was cold now. It was amazing how it happened. Miles kissed the water's surface once more. He hoped she would never leave him again. She had new friends and would never be alone ever again.

"My flowers, meet Elana. Mom, take care of her and Dad don't tell her any jokes," Miles said.

CHAPTER TWENTY-FOUR

LET THE BODIES FLOAT

Miles's dream felt so lifelike.

It was like he watched himself as he walked down a broken brick road. He didn't have ruby slippers, but everything was magnificent. With every step, different types of flowers, bright and bold, spouted from the road's cracks, then turned frail and faded to marble, flakes of snow fell from the cloudless blue sky as the sun beamed down, and warmed every inch of his skin. He saw someone in the distance. Something deep down told him to run, not away, but towards them. He had to see who it was.

As he approached them, they turned around slowly. It was Nora. She wore a long, flowing white dress splattered in red. She smiled at him with affection. He reached out to her, placed her hand inside his, and took him into her arms. Miles felt her skin. It was so soft and succulent beneath the goosebumps that perked up. Miles glided his thumb over her cherry red lips. Miles watched as her eyes glistened with fire that scorched his heart. When their lips met, they were trapped in a tornado. Ruining everything in their path.

The skies darkened, the snow turned into ash, the flowers wilted, the marble of the road cracked more, and no one existed. Except Miles and Nora. They looked down, Miles saw they stood on a pile of mangled, decaying bodies. The smiles they exchanged were the poison Miles had always longed for.

Miles embraced Nora and felt like a king with his perfect queen by his side.

"Rise and shine, boss," Davis said.

Miles woke and shielded his eyes from the sun as Davis came into focus.

"Davis?" Miles asked.

"Looks like we made it. And we're still standing," David said.

Miles got up and looked around. He didn't see Nora.

It really was a dream. And now the dream is gone.

Davis tried to move the heavy vases back into their places. He struggled. The more he tried, his face turned beet read. Miles felt a little stiff. He slept in one position all night, his back against the wall while he sat up, and Nora in his lap.

"Do you want some help?" Miles asked.

"Nope. I got it," Davis said as he lost his footing and slipped.

"You sure?" Miles asked.

"Yeah," Davis said as he tried again.

"Where's Nora and Renee?" Miles asked.

"Renee went to find something to eat, and Nora got a call and rushed out," Davis said.

"You got this for a minute?" Miles asked.

"Yep," Davis said with a strained voice.

Miles shook his head as he stepped outside. He breathed in the fresh air. Down the street, Renee was down the sidewalk with er hands full. Nora wasn't with her. The morning after a storm was Miles's favorite. He could still smell the rain in the air and felt like his sins had been washed away. Then he remembered he almost outed himself. He was so close. He did find it strange that the first time, he slept like a baby.

Nora, thank you for chasing the darkness away.

"Hey," Renee said

Before Miles could say anything back, Davis walked out. He was pale and looked like he was going to be sick. Miles knew something was wrong.

"Bae, what's wrong?" Renee asked.

"Hey, boss. I think you better come in and hear this," Davis said as he pointed inside.

To Miles's surprise the cable was working. Normally, it took days before it worked. Miles hopped up the steps and headed inside as Davis's eyes were glued to the television behind the front desk. On it, a reporter in dark blue sat with a line that streamed across it that said, *breaking news.*

"Don't tell me the alligators are loose again. Because if they are…" Renee said as she stepped behind them.

"It is one of the most shocking things ever to happen in New Orleans," the female reporter said.

"How many this time?" Renee asked.

"It's not an alligator," Davis said.

Renee placed everything on the counter and leaned next to Miles and watched.

"New Orleans police are overwhelmed, and some have stated in their career they have never been this shocked. Let's go to Robin LastName on the shore of Lake Conroe," the female reporter said.

A younger male reporter appeared on the split screen. In the background, police were everywhere. They were blocking the ever-growing audience, multiple reporters, the cameraman made sure to capture the audience's faces Then he zoomed in on police officers as they waded in the water, and some were bending down to the sand on the shore.

"Thank you, Cristina. Police are speechless right now. They received a call from a fisherman just before dawn who said he pulled up several articles of clothing including a black bra, underwear, along with long strands of hair. When he docked, he found what looked like a mannequin. But reports indicate that these are actually human remains that have washed up on the shore of Lake Conroe, which is right behind me," Robin said.

Holy mother of fuck me sideways. My garden.

"Are they sure it's not a prank?" Cristina asked.

"It's most definitely not a prank. The coroner has said this along with the Captain of the New Orleans Police Department," Robin said.

"Have they said what exactly they have found?" Cristina asked.

"No, they haven't but a source told me a fully intact hand with a silver bracelet with the initials E and S," Robin said.

Fuck! I thought I took it off. I never miss a thing. Ok, I grabbed the pillow and pressed down – I remember the jingle of her bracelet. Ok, think. I know I took it off. I had to.

Rounding the corner from the back room, Mom walked in. Miles saw the disappointment written all over her face. Her eyes were angry.

"You forgot about it," Mom said.

"There's no way," Miles said as he stared at her then back to the television.

"I know, I can't believe it either boss. Creepy," Davis said.

"Robin, has the captain made any kind of statement?" Cristina asked.

Nora's father is the captain.

"I think you have a problem," Mom said.

As she leaned on the counter next to Miles, she rubbed his back with her hand in a circle. She could tell he was stressed out. Miles knew he couldn't show it. It wasn't like Davis would catch on.

I did everything right.

"He has. Captain Thomas Asher stated that they are investigating…" Robin said.

Miles didn't understand how in the hell parts of her floated up. Between the alligators and other animals, there shouldn't have been anything left. Miles dropped his head on the counter and hit his forehead. This could be the end for him and Nora.

"I think I'm gonna be sick," Miles said.

"It's all right, baby boy. Everything is going to work out," Mom said.

"Look," Renee pointed to the television and said, "Some guy is running into the water."

Miles raised his head to see a man as he dropped to his knees in the water. He knew that man. It was Mr. Stansbury. Before he could react, the television cameras cut and a commercial popped on.

"Oh my god," Davis said.

"What. A. Drama. Queen," Mom giggled.

Davis placed his hand on Miles's shoulder and said, "I'm so sorry, boss"

I can't be the only serial killer living in New Orleans. I'm just the dumbest one.

CHAPTER TWENTY-FIVE

THE RANT

It had been three days since Miles last talked to Nora and seen her on the news. Miles was worried everything was too much for her after the police came to his shop and asked him questions. The multiple phone calls. It was crazy. And it was only going to get worse if Miles's garden was found. So far it hadn't been.

Miles slammed his office door. It felt good, especially after he slapped an empty coffee cup off his desk. It hit the wall. Miles braced his hands on the top of a filing cabinet, which turned his knuckles white. He repeatedly kicked the bottom of it until a dent started to form.

"For Christ's sake calm the fuck down," Mom said.

"I am calm," Miles said, breathless and angry.

"Uh, ok. Said the dent," mom said.

"Here we go. I can't wait to hear this. Where's a knife when you need one?" Miles snapped.

She leaned forward, rested her elbows on the edge of the desk, and picked up a small silver ball from my Newton's Cradle. She let it go, and they began to hit each other. It reminded Miles of the time he was playing the piano.

***

Miles nine-year-old hands tickled the ivory as mom kept in beat with the timer, which are these silver metal balls that sat right in front of him. A cool breeze flowed through the window and hit the sheet music, which sent them off and onto the floor.

"I guess the good lord wants you to have a break," mom said.

"But I wanna keep playing, for you momma," Miles said.

"Awe, my dedicated baby boy," mom said as she cupped Miles's face.

She stood. She held out her hand. Miles could smell the baby lotion she put on earlier that morning.

"Come on, I bet your father would love to hear how you have progressed," mom said.

Miles took it, she led him through the bright kitchen and out the back door. She looked back at him, the sun started to block her out and they walked into a dark shadow.

***

Miles stepped over and stopped the clicking sound. Unamused, she sat back and caressed the arms of the brown leather chair.

I know that grin. It's not, oh this is nice or where did you get it, she is doing the same thing I am. Remembering.

"Penny for your thoughts?" Miles asked as he took the seat across from her.

The glee in her eyes is brighter than any diamond a girl could ever have. She's thinking about him.

Like a widow spider, her fingers walked up and down the chair's arm, and left indents that were powerful and now everlasting.

"I thought we got rid of all his things. I can't believe you have it," mom said.

"I fished it out before the flames consumed it," Miles said.

"I remember like it was yesterday. And it was a GLORIOUS DAY," mom said as she twirled around.

"Good. Great. I prefer not to relive the past." Miles said.

"Come on, Miles. You have to admit the rush is pure ecstasy," mom said.

Not the words I would use, but she isn't the same person she used to be.

"Can we deal with the issue at hand? Please," Miles said.

"Fine," mom said.

"Get over yourself, mom," Miles said.

Thank you, mother, for another wonderful example of motherhood with your sarcastic attitude. It said so much to Miles as she stopped dead in her twirl and threw her leg on top of the light-colored wooden desk. Miles wanted her to be like, "hey, son, let's figure this out together." Miles wasn't surprised, she had always made things about herself. Her *it's all about me and how I feel* ways, Miles dealt with it his whole life.

Finally he snapped.

"I'm the one who is waiting for the cops to bust down my door. Mr. Stansbury was smiling behind the clear window of a prison, happy—no, vindicated—for his precious daughter's death. Oops, my bad. No mother. Let's deal with how YOU feel. FUCK ME," Miles said.

He stood in a huff, and she laughed.

"Stop acting like a child. Life doesn't imitate every Taylor Swift song. For fucks sake," Mom said.

"I had it. I had this amazing life in the palm of m hands, and you fucking ruined it," Miles said.

"Are you delusional or just fucking crazy? You were in a relationship with someone who was using you because of her father, which is fucking weird. That was no a relationship. I don't know what the fuck it was, but it wasn't the life I wanted you to live," mom said.

"But it was my life, and I was happy," Miles said.

"Blah, blah, blah. You sound just like your father. Speaking of your father. Have you visited him lately?" mom asked.

Now, she asks. It's been years.

"No, I haven't. Besides you hated him just as much as he hated you," Miles said.

"Ni I never hated him. I loved him. I hated what he did. You remember, you were there," mom said.

***

Miles sat on the top stairs and listened as his mother and father argued about his drinking. Again.

"You can't just leave and spend everything we have at the bar and on her," mom said.

"Don't tell me how what to do. I make the money, so I can do whatever I want," dad said.

"You have a family," mom said.

Miles hear desperation in her voice.

"Don't remind me," dad said.

"What is that supposed to mean?" mom asked.

"You know what I mean. If you didn't fuck every delivery guy, then I wouldn't have this problem," dad said.

"Who? Miles?" mom asked.

"Who else? I know he's not mine. I never wanted children, and you knew that," dad said.

"I can't help every time you came home from the bar you fucked me," mom said.

"Just to let you know. I was picturing a much younger, big-titted, and skinny bitch when I was with you," dad said.

Miles held onto the hourglass staircase bars; he winced as he heard mom cry out as his dad slapped her. He heard a crash. In the distance, something was coming closer, the thuds were loud and heavy, dad rounded the corner and stomped up the stairs. He never looked at Miles. Miles knew that he truly hated him. There was hate in his dad's eyes, and it scared Miles. He saw his mom as she stumbled and leaned in the foyer doorway. She had blood from a cut on her cheek. Miles knew that his dad wore a ring with sharp edges, and now it marked his something. She walked right up to Miles. She bent down.

"Did he hurt you?" mom asked.

Miles nodded, no.

"Don't worry baby boy. Mommy is going to fix all of this. Tonight," mom said she as embraced Miles. Miles loved him his mom hugged him. She gave the best hugs. She pulled back and looked into his eyes. "But I need your help. Will you help, mommy?"

Miles nodded yes. Then his mom smiled and reembraced him

***

"Oh, give me a break," Miles said as he paced.

"It's true," mom said.

No, I'm not falling for it again. I refuse. Nope. I can't. Not this time.

"Don't look at me all innocent and put this on me," Miles said with a furrowed brow.

"Well…" Mom said.

Miles pointed at her, and said, "Don't say it."

"I did what any mother would do," mom said.

"Shut up! I don't want to hear it," Miles said.

***

Miles's dad snored deep and loud. It always happened after a night of drinking. He came home, argued with mom, as usual he hit, and then crawled into bed. It was the same old, same old. *Miles's silhouette stood motionless, as his dark brown eyes stared at his dad. Mom placed her hand on my shoulder as she stepped behind Miles. He felt her hand tighten with every snore his dad made.*

"*Now remember what I taught you,*" *mom whispered.*

They walked slowly and quietly to the edge of the bed. She slid her hand down Miles's arm, lifted, and helped him aim the nine-millimeter at his dad. He snored again, and startled Miles, stepped back into his mom. But she was stone. Her cotton dress engulfed him as he tried to bury his head, not wanting to look at his dad.

She pulled him from her and with watery eyes she bent down to match Miles's size.

"*You said you were going to help me. Was that a lie?*" *mom asked.*

Miles shook his head no. Tears welled up in his eyes.

"Then you have to be the little man I have raised you to be," mom said.

She turned him back around and placed the gun back into his little hands. He hesitated, but she forced his hand together and forward over the gun. Her kips were not far from his ear, when she whispered soft and low not to wake Miles's dad.

"No squinting. Keep both eyes open," mom said.

Her hands were warm as she placed then over his to the gun in place because Mile's shook with fear. He started to cry. He was scared. He didn't want to and couldn't do this. Miles thought, what if dad woke up. What would he do to them. His mom. Would he beat both of them.

"Just think when this is all over. He will never hurt either of us again," mom said.

"I can't," Miles whimpered.

"Yes. You. Can. Think about silence. Remember the rules I taught you. Those who break them need to pay for their sins. Don't you love me?" mom asked.

"I do mommy," Miles said.

He took aim. He gripped the handle of the gun tight as his mom stepped back. Miles watched as his dad rolled onto his side. Miles imagined his dad would open his dark brown eyes. Miles stared at the shadow of darkness which flowed like a stream and covered his dad's face so he didn't have to see his reaction to what Miles was about to do.

Miles pulled back the trigger. A loud bang filled the room. Miles's dad's hand dropped and hung over the edge of the bed. The back of the wall was splattered with red as pieces of brain fell from it.

Back to reality, Miles was repeatedly clicking the trigger, but nothing came out. There were no bullets. He learned his mom had never loaded it. She tricked him. Tears streamed down his cheeks. His mom stepped in behind him once again and took the gun from my hand. Miles turned and fell into her.

"That's my baby boy," mom said.

She pulled him back and bent his head up to her with his chin.

"Who wants some ice cream? Do you want some ice cream? I have your favorite. The swirl kind," mom said.

His mom retrieved the gun from his little hand and placed it on the bedside table. Miles knew she tested his loyalty and commitment to her and to whom I love most. Hand in hand, they walked out.

"Oh, I have chocolate syrup too. I know how much you love it," mom said.

***

"I WAS A CHILD!" Miles said.

"You have always been half the man he was. Even when you were little," mom said.

"I did what you told me to do," Miles said.

"And you proved so much to me that night," mom said.

Manipulation is an extremely effective tool, especially when it comes to children. It either strengthens or weakens your relationship with your parent.

"And you have no problem with how I turned out," Miles said.

"I think you turned out great," mom said.

"I'm FUCKED UP!" Miles said.

"No, you're eccentric," mom said.

"Are you insane? I'm a serial killer who kills women who aren't the perfect partner," Miles said.

"Call it a divorce," mom said.

I can't – I don't even know what to say right now. No, I know.

"FUCK YOU!" Miles screamed.

She threw back Miles's dad's chair so hard it slammed into the wall and charged him. Miles stumbled backward. The rage in her eyes is the same as his. Miles saw where he got it now. But deep down he had always known.

"I raised you to be strong. Not a pussy. I gave you everything. As you were born, you ripped and damaged every part of me. I have never held that against you. Have I? Have I?" mom asked.

Miles agreed with a nod. He hated it when she was like this. Miles thought he just had to mention his dad had to mention his dad. He knew it was going to start a fight with her.

God help me. I'm just like her.

She raised her hand into the air, and Miles winced. She noticed and the rage faded. She became the mother he loved.

"Oh, I'm sorry. Sometimes I forget how fragile you can be. I just hate when you blame me for what you did," mom said.

She run her fingers through Miles's hair. It reminded him of when, years later, Miles found out how his father died. He was shot and robbed while on his way from card game.

"I'm sorry, " mom said.

Shaking, she took him into her arms, held him tight, and said, "Don't worry, baby boy. Everything is going to be all right. I promise. It always works out."

Miles pulled back.

"So, what do I do now?" Miles asked.

"You have to find out what she knows. And – I know you're not going to like this. But you will have to," mom said.

"Send her to the bottom." Miles finished her sentence.

CHAPTER TWENTY-SIX

WHO IS NORA ASHER, REALLY?

He knew Nora wasn't home, which made it easier for him to break in. It was a good thing the neighbors were having a party next door. It made it easier for Miles to blend in, laugh with the guys as he made his way to Nora's front door.

"Ha, yeah, I know, bro. Tell me more about the girl you were hitting on last night," Miles shouted over the loud music.

At Nora's door, he took out the lock pick he got online. He quietly thanked the hunting shop he ordered from. It was amazing what he learned in fifteen minutes from a video. He turned it a few times, then he heard it unlock. He opened the steel sliding door slowly and kept an eye out on neighbors.

He wrapped his hands around the edge. He slid it open enough to slide half in. He stopped. He felt something on the inner part of the door. Miles thought how smart Nora was. It was tape. Miles smiled. Nora set a trap. He was impressed.

Note to self: replace the tape before I leave.

You have respect for everything, everyone, and yourself. Zoe didn't. The lack of it is the reason she was the fourth.

I should have told you everything, but I can't — I was. I believe I was. We had a moment the other night. Look, I know that this is going to be hard for both of us. But in the end, I think we will be better off. Nora, you will be closer to me than you were. But first I have to know what's been going on.

***

As Miles rushed around Zoe's apartment cleaning up the place, Zoe laid upside down in the blue chair Miles bought her for her birthday. Early of course because he was like that. And he loved to see her smile.

"Please get off your phone before everyone gets here," Miles said as he continued to gather clothes in a small basket.

"I told you I never wanted a party, let alone have to clean the place up for it. You're on your own," Zoe said.

He looked at the clock on the wall. The hour he gave himself to clean up was going to go by quickly. It was going to take a U-Haul and at least seventeen cans of Lysol to just freshen the place up.

"Zoe, please at least do the dishes so we have clean..." Miles said.

As Zoe flipped around, she smiled at her phone. Miles leaned over and saw she was too busy to talk or do anything because she was on level two hundred and six of her puzzle block game. Miles hated that game.

She was always on it. Even when Miles wanted to have some personal time, she was on that phone. He hated that phone.

"Can't we cancel this thing and do it like next year? I'm almost at level 1692," Zoe asked.

"No. No. It's been planned for weeks," Miles said.

Frustrated, he dropped the laundry basket on the magazine table. The one she never cleaned. Does she ever clean? He waited for her reaction. He listened to the blocks as they hit each other, and Zoe didn't move. Miles cleaned his throat. Zoe scoffed as she stood. She looked at Mile as if to say I don't have to do anything. Then she walked past him.

"Where are you going?" Miles asked,

"Anywhere but here," Zoe said as she headed to the front door.

She's not going anywhere looking like that, Miles thought. She doesn't even respect herself, Miles stared down at her clothes. He hated her self-made holes with scissors, stains on her shirt and her hair tossed up in a bun. Messy bun, but not the cute messy bun most women do if they are going out or have spontaneous guests. Zoe. Shoes. Uh, it was called tenuous if you step on a rusty nail, or you might get a splinter.

"I deserve better," Zoe said.

Excuse me? You deserve better, What about me? I want to be with someone who doesn't see me as a maid or a mommy. You're not going anywhere.

Zoe began to open the door, when Miles slammed it shut, which caught her fingers, and she screamed. Miles backhanded her, and she stumbled backward and tripped over her big brown purse onto the ground. She never had time to react. Miles straddled her. He placed both of his hands on either side of her head and banged her head onto the wooden floor.

Miles lost count as in the French-speaking film played in the background. The music from is made Miles the star of the film. Zoe went *limp and a small pool of blood formed under her dusty blonde hair. Her ivory skin was sprinkled with red, and he looked around.*

Miles always got stuck with the cleaning.

***

Back and forth, Miles shone his flashlight around. The place was perfect. It wasn't just clean but spotless. It was the kind of clean that a stay-at-home mom wished they had. He stopped at the mantel and ran his fingers over the photos displayed. In the last picture were Nora, her brothers, and Kelly, the sister he learned about at the barbecue.

The room reminded him of an operating room or a morgue. It felt cold and distant, yet somehow still homey. The couch pillows are positioned with military-like precision, each featuring a perfect six-inch chopped indentation. The furniture legs align perfectly with the wild, wavy lines of the rug, creating an almost choreographed visual harmony.

The moonlight streamed through bright white blinds, casting a perfect shadow across the coffee table, cushions, and wall. He was impressed.

Examining her movie collection revealed a telling profile—mostly horror films, arranged meticulously in alphabetical order. The true fascination emerged with the serial killer documentaries. The Zodiac Killer, Ted Bundy, John Wayne Gacy, the Green River Killer, Cropsey, H.H. Holmes, and every season of *Dexter* lined the shelves. Clearly, rom-coms are not Nora's style—unless someone dies.

With music in the background from the party, he walked into the kitchen. The counter was cold to the touch but hard and firm. Take-out containers filled the fridge, but he didn't know how long they had been in there. Miles chuckled after he found strawberries, whipped cream, and Tabasco sauce were the staples in her refrigerator.

What I wouldn't give to have you laying on it with barely anything on. Let's throw some strawberries into the mix. As you can see-

"So, are you going to just stand there, or are you going to do something?" mom said.

"I'm just looking. No harm in that. I can get to know her a little bit better and..." Miles said.

"And getting fingerprints all over the place. Let alone time is somewhat of an option here, Miles," mom said.

"Thank you for the reminder, Mother," Miles said.

"She could walk in anytime and we are done for," Mom said.

Miles understood the disconnect in her statement about "we." If he got caught, he would take the blame to protect her. She knew that. There hadn't been a genuine "we" between them for a long time, but he understood her overprotective nature. His mother rolled her eyes, seemingly bothered by his presence.

Miles knew he was wasting time, and oddly, he was fine with that. He wished she wasn't there, though he recognized her occasional annoyingness.

"I'm going to the bathroom. Maybe I'll wear Secret or Dove," his mother announced, walking backward into the living room.

He couldn't help but smile at her enthusiasm.

"Come on, Miles. I can drop the top," Nora said.

Yes, no, yes. He tried to focus, to remember his original purpose. But Nora's image kept popping in with less clothing.

Her voice, slow and seductive, rushed through his veins.

"Don't you want to play with me, Miles Pike?" Nora asked.

And then she was naked.

Miles braced himself against the door frame, his imagination running wild with increasingly explicit scenarios involving Nora.

Opening her drawers, Miles tossed out her sweatpants and bras.

What was that? A phone. Miles tried to convince himself it was normal to have two phones.

So, I'm going to freak out about this. One for personal use and one for work. But Nora is at work. There's only one thing I can do to see which phone this is. I'll text her: I was wondering if you wanted to catch a coffee after work tonight or in the morning.

"Two phones, huh, she's a cop," Mom said.

"Crime scene photographer," Miles said.

"For the cops. Seriously, honey, don't think with your dick," Mom said.

Miles shook his head annoyed at his mom as he slid his finger across the screen, wondering if she had a lock and a code that he would be able to figure out. To his surprise, he was in. He scrolled through the contents but found nothing—absolutely nothing.

Miles watched as his mom flopped down on the edge of Nora's bed, and bounced on it like a little kid. It was funny to see.

"There's nothing here. Maybe we jumped the gun," Miles said.

"Whatever you say," mom said.

Miles's phone dinged. He got a text back from Nora. It read, *looks like I'm coming down with something. I'm going to crawl into bed and sleep it off. I'll call you tomorrow.*

"Oh, I know that look," mom said.

As Miles started to text Nora back, something caught his eye. He lowered himself down and inched his way toward the corner of Nora's bed. He placed his phone back inside his pocket, reached for it and pulled on a folder. And as soon as he pulled it out, a bunch of pictures fell out.

Spread all over the floor were pictures of Miles. His eyes danced from one place to another at a rapid pace. One was one was him as he sat outside the coffee shop down by his work, biting into a beignet, and the other is opening Petal Perfection as he pulled the heavy silver gate up. As he stepped around them, he saw a few pictures of him and Heathcliff at the restaurant, and a few of him the night he dumped Fairy in the lake.

Miles bent down, picked up the picture of him as he returned to the dock without Fairy's body, his hand shook. His mom peered over his shoulder.

"Some of these were taken before Nora and I ever met," Miles responded as he stared at the pictures.

Nora has been at this for a long time. I don't even own that shirt now.

"If you're right then that means …" mom said.

"She's been watching me for a long time," Miles said.

"I knew something was wrong with her," mom said.

I swear, mother is more neurotic and bipolar dead than she was alive. But I have to know what else is under there.

Miles dropped on all fours and looked back under Nora's bed. At first, there was nothing but darkness, but then he noticed something pushed all the way to the back. He reached for the flat, clear binding with his fingers. No, luck. He rolled onto his back and stretched his arms as far as they could go. Still skimming the edge, he moved it just enough to grab it. He stood up. He took hold of the bed and pulled it to one side.

CHAPTER TWENTY SEVEN

SHE KNOWS

For the first time in his life, Miles understood what the saying "a fish out of water" meant. He imagined a fish lying on the floor as it gasped for air. Dying. It hoped for someone to pick it up and put it back in its tank. Miles stepped alongside his mom and stared down at an enormous board. He couldn't believe what he saw.

A black and white photo of him was pinned in the center. Underneath, written on several large index cards, was his daily schedule for the last two years. His eyes darted around the board as he checked out the pictures. Miles was drinking an iced coffee, walking down the sidewalk, eating a powdered doughnut, seated on a bench near the lake, and in his apartment. The last few were a story he only silently told to Nora and Miles as he entered the building with roses. The next was him as he stood in front of the door. Then he saw Elana, before and after her death.

It was a gallery of not just Miles, but of all of his girlfriends, with the bold letters, *Garden of Girls*.

Long, straight lines of red yarn run from me to other pictures. The pictures feature Miles's past—Abbey, Jenna, Chloe, Zoe—their brown, blue, hazel, and green eyes looking back at him. Each photo is marked with the date we met and the date they left or disappeared, with question marks at the end.

How the fuck does Nora know about them?

Miles had covered all his tracks or at least he thought he did. Adrenaline pumped through him as he paced back and forth so fast it was becoming his blood. His heart was turning to stone.

"I trusted her. I wanted her. I wanted her," Miles said.

There's no way this is happening to me. Fuck!

"You have to calm down," mom said.

"Calm down! How? She's been watching me - FUCK!" Miles said as he punched the wall.

"We can fix this. We have to before she does something stupid," mom said.

"Before - I think she already has. Look at this. Every step, place, person - she knows. I'm done for. It's over," Miles said.

"Get rid of it," mom said.

She's gone mad again.

"I can't just get rid of it," Miles said.

"Why not?" mom asked.

"Because she might have copies or something like that," Miles said.

"Then what are you waiting for?" mom asked.

Miles flung open her closet and went through Nora's clothes. He thought of his garden. Zoe, he did what he had to do. Jenna, she deserved it. Elana. She was the best thing to ever happen to him in his life. He ended it horribly. It didn't matter. He empties each drawer, letting it slip from his fingers. He doesn't care if they break. He was broken. *Oh my god, how does she know*? He had to do something. Stopping, he leaned against the wall and slid down. He pulled his knees to his chest and hoped the pain would stop. But it didn't. He had never felt this way before. His chest tightened...

Granted I have intruded into Nora's place. I feel violated. Funny how the tides turn. I thought I was watching her – she was investigating me. Why?

Miles felt her cold hands cradle his cheeks. He looked into her eyes and knew exactly what she was saying before she even said a word.

She's right. Nora wouldn't make anything easy. She's not easy. She's complicated. She's not as open as I thought she was. Looks like a game to me. Maybe this is what it is. Finding the board of me was easy. The kitchen.

Miles opened the cabinets and then traced his fingers over everything. Nora wasn't stupid. She wouldn't leave anything or even a hint.

"What about a dark room? Photographers have those," mom said.

"Her place isn't big enough for one. Besides, I know she would have mentioned it." Miles said.

But if she *did* have one, it had to be hidden. But she would hide them inside something. Miles pulled out all the drawers and tossed out the silverware — false bottoms. He picked each one up and slammed it down onto the counter. Empty. Empty. He searched through another, and the bottom was loose. He pulled at the corner of it but couldn't get it. He used a butcher knife and finished the break. He found nothing.

"Think about the first time you met her," mom said.

"It was at the coffee shop," Miles said.

"What a perfect opportunity to meet you," mom said.

Miles thought about it and concluded that his mom was right. Nora meant to run into him. She must have seen him and taken the opportunity when Miles wasn't paying attention. Maybe Nora it was because of Nora he tripped over the woman's purse strap. It would have been easy for her to slip it off.

After all these years, she had to meet me. Wanted to meet me. Why? You lied to me, Nora.

CHAPTER TWENTY-EIGHT

CONFESSION FOR BOTH

As Miles sat in the dark in the dark blue chair, he listened to the boom of the music from next door He couldn't help but keep his eyes off Nora's picture, which he had in his hand. A wave of nostalgia washed over him, mixed with a tinge of rage. He remembered the times he and Nora had spent together. His heart was heavy with the realization that those moments were now just distant memories. He crumpled her picture and tossed it onto the floor. He heard the jingle of keys. He looked up as Nora walked in. He wanted to be the first thing she saw. His leg shook nervously, not because he was scared but because he was angry.

"Remember it's not *who* she is but *what* she is, police or not," mom says.

Nora enters.

"I broke my rules for you," Miles said.

Startled, Nora jumped after she heard his voice.

Oh, you're scared. Too little, too late. I'm not buying it. I found everything, Nora. The act is over.

Miles turned the lamp on beside him and stared at her.

"Fuck, Miles. You scared the shit out of me," Nora said. She placed her gun back in its holster. "What are you doing here? I thought…"

"You thought what? I was some crazed, mad lunatic – or are you hoping I am. Because your little project makes me out to be," Miles said, calm and strong.

"What in the hell are you talking about" Nora asked.

"Your little map. Of me and my exes. The one under your bed," Miles said.

She glanced toward her room and then sat down at the kitchen counter. Miles saw a wave of relief. *Strange.* If this had happened to Miles, he was sure he would have snapped by now. Maybe even taken a shot. She made him more interested in her.

"How do you know Elana?" Miles asked as he held her picture up.

Let me guess, Nora. You're going to stumble over your words. Act like you have no idea how or what this picture is. I've seen enough movies to know how this is going to play out. But please give it your best shot before I snap your neck and rip your head from your body with my bare hands.

"I was wondering what was taking you so long," Nora said.

No, you're supposed to be shocked and confused, Nora. Not relieved. But the game is up, so you might as well – tell the truth.

"The first week I expected you to find everything. But wow. You surprised me," Nora said.

Nora walked nonchalantly over to the refrigerator, pulled it open, and grabbed a bottle of water. She leaned on the counter after taking a long sip.

What is happening here? Nora is calm and cool – is she thrilled to see me?

"Ok. I'm ready," Nora said. "Shoot. I'll answer anything you want."

I'll bite.

"Elana?" Miles asked as he held up her picture again.

"Well, that's simple. We were roommates at prep school. She was the popular girl who was always high as a kite, and I was the one she paid for tests and do her assignments. Nothing more," Nora said.

"And?" Miles asked.

"And what?" Nora asked.

He shook the picture which made Nora laugh as she walked around the counter. She picked up the barstool Miles had knocked over.

"You didn't have to trash the place," Nora said.

"I was a little upset," Miles said.

Miles felt her stare penetrate him as she walked her fingers along the stool's edge. She smirked.

"I said I would answer your questions. But I have a feeling I'm supposed to just tell you," Nora said.

That's the plan. So, spill, Nora.

"I believe you owe me," Miles said.

"Fair enough. That particular picture was taken by Fairy. I'm surprised it even came out the way she lifted my camera and hit the button. Fairy never cared for me. She thought I was this scrawny, good for nothing scholarship kid. And she was right on the scrawny part, but the scholarship," Nora said.

A personal tie.

"I was supposed to be payback for all the cruelty Elana put you through," Miles said.

Somehow, I understood it.

"Well, not exactly. You were and are more like a bonus in the game of bully roulette. So, to speak," Nora said as she bobbed her head back and forth.

"How long have you known about me?" Miles asked.

"Two years," Nora said.

"Care to elaborate a little? I mean with all the hard work you've put in on your board. I have to hear your amazing story of discovery and wonderment," Miles said.

"Well, if we are going to be like that. I'll be more than happy to tell you. I was at the lake – Lake Conroe – down a-little ways where the docks are. And I was thinking about Elana, my job, family...you. Then out of the blue, I saw headlights. Someone got out and pulled out a large, long shower curtain. Curiosity killed the cat, so I followed them. Hell, I didn't know what was happening until," Nora said.

An arm fell out as I loaded her inside the rowboat.

"To my surprise, it was you, Miles," Nora said.

No doubt she knows about Elana. And Fairy. Here I am thinking it was Chet the entire time who saw me, but it was her.

"I watched you do everything. You dumped her in, I saw you blow a kiss as she sank and then leave. And you started your life all over again the next day. I was fascinated. I had to know more, I had to know you," Nora said.

I met Elana a few days later.

"There was this need deep inside that pulled me toward you. So, I began following you. Learning about everything. Your past girlfriends. I thought I would get to see what they were like and basically mimic them. I never found them. Then it hit me where they were. The lake," Nora said.

Miles looked at the gun. She followed my glare. Her sigh was heavy, and her head dropped.

"Cute family picture. A family of cops," Miles said.

"Thanks. Wanna know what I did that night?" Nora asked.

"Why not?" Miles said.

"I watched you and Elana fuck through the window. I have to say. I was turned on. And hated her even more because I wished it was me instead of her," Nora said.

Miles let Elana's picture fall from his hands. She pulled her collar back.

"Then I made a choice," Nora said.

Miles grabbed onto the chair's arms and squeezed it until his knuckles turned white. His mom's hand glided over the back of the chair and began to rub his shoulders. He stared at Nora as she smiled to herself.

"Fairy. That was amazing. I would have given anything to smash her face in up close," Nora said.

"She's like us, baby boy," mom said.

Miles heard pride in her voice.

"But you said I need to send her to the bottom," Miles said.

Nora sat up and looked at Miles with excitement. The heels of her shoes clicked on the floor. It echoed in Miles's mind as his heart pounded, and the rage began to surface from the deepest part of Miles. It slowly swallowed him.

"How did it feel? Giving that bitch what she was owed?" Nora asked.

Nora saw it. She didn't do it, so I'm the next best thing for feeling the thrill of taking Fairy's life. Desperation is one part to keep my secret. I have to tell her I was protecting her. Look at her smile. She's so happy.

"Good. It felt good," Miles said. "She knew about you."

Nora squealed with enjoyment. Miles's mom bent down. Her breathy whispers tickled his ear as she wrapped her arms around him.

When she was alive, comfort was all Miles ever wanted from her. In death, she gave it. But it was too little, too late.

"I remember the first time you did that. There's nothing like the rush of getting rid of a problem," mom said.

Problem? Fairy wasn't a problem she was a pain in my ass. I did what I had to – shit. Nora and I are the same through and through.

Miles's mom walked and sat next to Nora on the couch.

"She has quite an interesting story about it. I think you need to ask her – no wait even better. Wait until she offers the story. Because she will," mom said.

Nora got up. Miles shot his glare at the gun that was still on the kitchen counter. The way she gazed at Miles; it melted him. He shook it off because this was about survival. His survival. It had always been him verses everyone else, but this time he was against Nora. How could this have happened? He knew love blinded him. He hd to remember that she knew everything about him. She picked up one of her Ted Bundy documentaries and tapped it. It was damaged from Miles after he destroyed it along with the others.

"This one was my favorite," Nora said.

She flung it across the room like it was nothing. It hit the wall. She chuckled.

"You owe me a new one," Nora said.

"Noted," Miles said.

"I was wondering if you have a collection like mine," Nora said.

Miles eyes widened a little once he heard that. Then he knew she had been at his place. He didn't know how many times, but it didn't matter. She had invaded his privacy. He hated that. He imagined her as she walked in, glided her fingers across the back of his couch, going through his things. She could have even worn some of his clothes. But most of all she knew his schedule. It made sense why he was short of a few bags of popcorn. He was excited at the thought of her on his bed, buried her face in his pillow, and inhaled Miles's scent like a predator on the hunt.

"Let's just say, if I did those things, and that those pictures were real and not AI or whatever the fuck kids do these days. Why would a cop want to learn from me? And why haven't you turned me in?" Miles asked.

"It's like that commercial after school that taught teens more about drugs, drinking and shit like that. The more you know. Well, it's true and the better you learn," Nora said.

Come on Nora. Don't dangle the carrot anymore.

"It's simple. Paul murdered my sister one night when she was trying to leave him when Alex was one. He ripped Alex from her arms, put him down and repeatedly beat Kelly until she quit moving. No weapons. Just his hands. She was in a coma for a few days and died – I was in the room when her heart stopped. As I cried, I looked up to see Paul through the window. His department covered it up because he's one of them. So, I became one to learn what not to do," Nora said.

She's from the wrong side of the tracks when it comes to the law. She doesn't give a shit about the oath she took. It's just another breath of air for her. Now it makes sense why there are so many serial killer docs. They are teaching her what NOT to do. She doesn't want to make a mistake. But she already is. She met me.

"I will never forget the smirk on his face as the nurses and doctor rushed in and tried to save her. When the doctor called it – Paul turned and walked away. My parents fought hard for Alex and instead of this coming back up, Paul gave my parents custody. But..." Nora said.

"Now he wants his son back," Miles said.

"Over my dead body is he going to get Alex back," Nora said.

She's angry. She means it too. She's not going to let this go until he's dead. I know the feeling.

"Why don't you let the law take care of this," Miles said.

She laughed.

"I have exhausted every avenue. I have been told that there isn't proof of it. He covered his tracks well. The law isn't going to help me or my family, especially Alex. So, I am," Nora said.

She never wanted to turn me in. She wants me to teach her how to get away with it.

"This isn't a game. People's lives aren't pieces on a board," Miles said.

Miles watched as Nora's breath sped up. He noticed her narrowed her eyes, and grinned as he knew he had offended her. Nora stood and turned her back to Miles.

"I counted twelve," Nora said.

No! She's been in the lake, explored my garden, counted my loves.

Miles leaned up, his upper lip trembled. He gripped the arm of the chair so hard he pierced the fabric. Outside the music continued to boom.

"You've been investigating me for two years, Nora," Miles said then screamed, "TWO FUCKING YEARS."

Startled, Nora jumped but recovered quickly. She pointed at her front door.

"Behind those doors will be at least six cops. They are coming to shut down the party. I guarantee you if I scream or anything happened to me, they will break down that door and put a fucking bullet in you," Nora said.

"I'm about three seconds from snapping your neck," Miles gritted through his teeth.

"I never intended to feel the way I feel about you."

I knew it. All the times she flirted with me, touched me, and even the moments when -

"This place could be bugged." mom said as her voice rose. "This could all be a setup."

Miles had to say something, but in his mind the background noise was so loud. He wondered about his girls and flooded with questions. *Did she do something to them? Did she take pictures with them? Are they alright?* He heard them call his name. They were afraid. But first, he had to handle Nora.

"Aren't you going to say anything?" Nora asked.

"There's no way she's just giving you all this information because of feelings. Baby boy, use your head. And not the other one," mom said as she appeared from nowhere.

"We're in too deep now," Miles said.

"I know, I know. I take the blame for this. I wanted to tell you, but the time has never been right," Nora said.

"I know," Miles said.

Nora stepped forward. Miles paced back and forth, while he tried to figure out what to do. But it was hard to listen as both talked at the same time. Their voices split his ears and sounded like chainsaws. At the same time, Nora and mom reached for him. Miles jerked back.

"Ask her. Ask her," mom continuously repeated.

"Bad time I know, but if you would listen to me," Nora said.

"I am!" Miles said at his mother.

I yelled. I'm sorry. But you have to understand the predicament you – both of you have put me in. I have to figure out how to save my own ass, but figure out whatever is between us, Nora, and deal with this fucked up situation. Mother fucker I wish the music would stop. I swear I'm about to come to unglued and shove the speaker down Nora's neighbor's throat.

"Will you both just shut the fuck up?!" Miles screamed.

"Both?" Nora asked.

Miles picked up the chair and tossed it across the room. When it hit the wall, it cracked. He lunged toward his mother. They hit one of the side tables and knocked over a glass vase. It broke on the floor on impact. Miles muffled his mom's screams as he wrapped his hands around her neck. She fought him. She tried to move and kick but Miles was too strong. Beside him a piece pf the broken vase flicked into his eyes. He grabbed it and gripped it so hard, it broke the skin of his palm. He placed it underneath his mom's chin.

"Do it. If it makes you feel better. But know I have never told anyone what you did," she said.

Nora?

CHAPTER TWENTY-NINE

TWO PEAS IN A POD

Nora had no hesitation about dying in Miles's hands. She gave him a loving smile. Her gaze was distant and cold. She was not the Nora he craved for, begged for, and needed every second of every day. She wasn't who he expected her to be.

She was *better*.

Nora grabbed his hand and started to push up. The glass's tip slowly pierced her skin. As Miles took a heavy breath, it was the first time he was next to her the way he had always wanted.

"Do it," Nora said.

She wants me to kill her. No, no, no – you don't, Nora. You're testing me. You want to see if how I feel about you is real or not. If I kill you, my life will return to normal. But I will lose her forever. If I don't, she will never leave my side. You mean more to me than my own life.

Sweat from Miles's brow fell onto her cheeks and slid down like a raindrop onto the floor. She licked her lips. Miles pushed the glass further. Then, Mile's thought, they were the same.

Nora wanted to be like Miles; he knew that. And he wanted to be with her to be normal. Blood dripped and flowed down the crease of Nora's neck.

Miles crawled off Nora and sat on his knees in front of her. Miles saw a sense of relief from her as she sat up. Her neck looked like a map. Now that he could actually feel pain, he winced and then dropped the glass onto the floor. It hurts like hell. Nora got up. She walked over into the kitchen and picked up a dish towel from the floor. She tossed the rag to Miles as she walked back over.

"Sorry about the mess," Miles said as he caught the towel, "I promise to help you clean up."

"You're damned right you will," Nora said.

He wrapped the towel around his hand with a wince. Nora flopped down beside him with a loud sigh. Miles noticed the blood on her neck.

I did that. I hurt her. I can't believe I hurt her. Please don't hold it against me, Nora. I should have – I don't know what I should have done. But I didn't have to lunge like that at you. Sometimes the beast inside takes over.

"Here," Miles said as he started to unfold his hand.

"No, you need it more than me," Nora said.

So, what do we do now, Nora? Clean? Sit here like a bunch of wild assholes. No, I'm the asshole. I need to apologize.

"I'm sorry," Miles said.

"Why are you apologizing? I'm the one who dumped all of this on you. I have always had bad timing," Nora said.

I think bad timing is not what this was.

"I should have been honest from the beginning. Instead, I became this secretive person who by the way knew it was coming to this," Nora said.

"Well, maybe not this way," Miles said.

I love her laugh.

"Let me see your hand," Nora said.

Nora carefully peeled back the blood-soaked towel and revealed a nasty gash in Miles's hand. She looked concerned. Miles was happy she was close to him. He never wanted any of this to happen. He wanted to have all his girls and secrets to himself. Now, Miles admitted to himself that there was something between them. He wasn't going to fight it any longer. Nora had been able to pull back his layers and saw the real me.

I really made a mess of things. But there is a way to make it up to her. Give her what she wants.

"Looks like you're going to need a few stitches," Nora said.

"It'll heal. They always do," Miles said.

"I have some butterfly strips. I'll get them," Nora said.

She started to get up, but Miles grabbed her arms and dragged her back down onto the floor.

He examined her face. Nora didn't know what he was doing. His lifted bloody hand and caressed her cheek. In Miles's mind, he had marked her. He had never felt so deeply in my entire life. Miles was as calm as one can be for almost murdering the love of his life. He breathed deeply and noticed he was happier than he had ever been, leaning into her. She closed her eyes as she gripped his hand and laced his blood between her fingers.

Miles closed his eyes, and Nora did the same as they laid their foreheads together and just sat together.

"I will help you," Miles said.

"I knew you would. Miles, I..." Nora said.

"I know," Miles said.

CHAPTER THIRTY

FIRST COME, FIRST SERVES, ANOTHER DEATH

For a Saturday night in 'Nawlins, the street is strangely quiet. That's also a good thing. Soon it wouldn't be when Mardi Gras started. Miles and Nora parked across the street from a dark house with only one light that shone in the second-story window. Miles looked at Nora, she looked like a beast ready to devour its prey. Her look reminded him of the plan.

***

Nora and Miles gazed at a drawing of her brother-in-law's house.

"No guns. No knives. No weapons," Miles said.

"Because they can be traced. Especially if a bullet is found. Plus filing the number on them is a bitch," Nora said.

"And knives can be traced because they are collected if anything is suspected," Miles said.

"So, what do we use?" Nora asked.

"These," Miles said.

Miles help up his hands.

***

Nora pointed to a room upstairs and then guided her finger to the living room.

"His bedroom is here. But he sleeps on the couch most of the time. He's a heavy drinker," Nora said.

"Good, if he's drinking. But we have to think he'll be sober in order to make it through this - rough plan," Nora said.

***

Nora made nine red circles on the makeshift map.

"I don't have all night. If you want this done tonight, then you must be right on this. Time is an issue," Miles said.

"Twenty-five seconds," Nora said.

"Are you sure?" Miles asked.

Miles could see Nora thinking the wheels in her head were doing double time.

"Nora, are you sure?" Miles asked.

"Yeah. Yes. Twenty-five seconds," Nora said.

"You need..." Miles said.

Nora slams her hand down. Hard.

"I'm sure," Nora said.

"All right," Miles said.

***

Seven and a half seconds. To Miles, that was close enough. They made their way to the back door. It was locked. Miles should have known. He bent down, took out his lock pick, and got to work. Miles basically had fifteen seconds. For some people, that was not enough time, but it was, and the easiest part for Miles. Nora maintained her gaze on the camera as it began to rotate. She tapped his shoulder. Miles didn't react as he kept his head in the game. It unlocked. They rushed in as fast as they could. As the camera pointed to the door, Miles shut it quickly and quietly.

"That was close," Nora whispered.

Too fucking close. Note to self: don't touch a thing.

Miles hated this guy already. The small waste basket was full of crushed beer cans. Miles was impressed, and he wondered how someone could drink that much. Miles can't believe he's still alive. For now.

***

They were surrounded by staleness and silence, which was disturbing. Miles liked disturbing; he thrived on it, but this was out of his comfort zone. He couldn't believe Paul lived this well. From what Nora told him; Kelly was the breadwinner and paid for the house. If he wasn't about to murder Paul, he would have suggested he hire a fucking maid or call the CDC. Miles glanced around and thought, fuck it. He might as well burn the place down himself.

Nora motioned toward the staircase. Magazines, books, and more beer bottles are on every other step. Miles saw something that resembled slime. He didn't really want to know; as long as he didn't have to touch it, he was fine. Quietly, they made their way around the stairs toward the foyer when they saw a pair of headlights turn into the driveway. They have no choice but to split up. Nora dashed upstairs and rounded the corner into a room. Miles made a mad rush around the stairs and into a small coat closet. But not before he bumped into a side table and a vase of rocks. He watched in horror as it began to fall as the front door opened. Miles had no choice as he ran toward it and grabbed it. He placed it back on the stand and slammed his body against the wall in the living room.

The front door slammed.

Shit!

Miles's reflection was staring back at him through a large empty picture frame. Miles was in perfect position.

Better me, than Nora. I hope she's okay.

Paul walked in, tossed his things in the corner, and simply stood as he lit another cigarette, The smoke made him squint as it went into his eyes. As he exhaled, he lets out a long, loud sigh. He was surrounded by smoke.

"Strange thing," Paul hollered out.

Paul stepped outward, his police issue boots hitting heavily on the floor. He took another drag. Miles peered at him and saw a loser; a dangerous loser.

"I was at work when my silent alarm went off," Paul said.

Silent alarm. One thing neither of us thought of. This isn't going to be good. I have to get to Nora before he does.

Paul dropped his cigarette onto the floor and put it out with the tip of his boot. As he was about to make his move, Miles snapped his stare upstairs when he heard a bang. Miles turned back to Paul, who grinned. Paul's smile was sly and disgusting, and Miles wanted to take each little yellowing tooth with a pair of rusty pliers.

"Here kitty, kitty. I love a good game of hide-and-seek. I hunted your sister and now it's your turn," Paul said as he made his way toward the stairs.

"You found me," Nora said as she appeared at the top of the landing.

Miles knew she had lost her mind. Instantly, he grabbed the vase he almost knocked over. He turned the corner out from the living room back into the foyer. Miles rushed and crashed the vase over Paul's head. Pieces fell onto the steps, Paul turned and leered at me.

"Assaulting a police officer is the dumbest thing you can do. Assaulting me? The deadliest thing you could do," Paul said.

Paul pushed Miles backward. Miles tried to grab something to regain his balance, but there was nothing. He never felt it as he flew through the air. He landed on my back, and my head bounced. Miles was knocked out.

Miles came too. He could hear blend of grunts and screams. He knew it was Nora, but sounded like she was deep inside a tunnel. Miles's vision was blurry. And the back of his head throbbed. He touched the back of my head and saw blook on his fingertips. He heard another scream. Head spinning, he used the staircase pulled himself up.

He glanced over his shoulder and saw Nora. She was blurry. Miles shook his head in the hope it would wake him up. As my vision came back, the ringing stopped Nora gasped for air. Paul slammed her against the living room doorframe with his hands around her throat.

Miles lost his balance a few times and fell. He saw as Paul jerked Nora up, placed her in a headlock, which forced her to her knees.

"I love a girl on her knees," Paul said.

Nora faced Miles as she hit and struggled in Paul's hands, never able to break his grip. The look on his face said it all. He was enjoying every second. With everything Miles had, he rushed at him. He ran into Paul's foot as he kicked out. *He's strong and tough.* Miles landed on the ground hard. But then, like some miracle, an open letter landed beside him. He grabbed it.

As Miles screamed and lunged forward, the letter opener slid into Paul's neck. Miles took it out and stabbed him in the back until he released Nora. After he did, she scrambled away and braced herself against the wall in the living room while she gasped for air. Paul stumbled backward. Miles wasn't going to let him off that easily. Repeatedly, he jammed the letter open a few more times into Paul's neck.

"I'm not going to be the last one you see before I send you to hell," Miles said.

Miles turned his head towards Nora as he held out the bloody letter opener. Nora's breathing calmed as she placed her hand on the floor. Blood slowly pooled under Paul as he reached out. Nora took the letter opened from Miles, who graciously stepped to the side. Nora slapped Paul's hand away. Miles slid back a few feet to admire Nora. He was so proud of her.

"This is for my sister, you son-of-a-bitch," Nora said.

Nora stabbed Paul in the neck one last time. She wasn't done with him yet, as Miles thought. He watched as she stomped on him, from his foot to his head. Paul was finally getting what he deserved. And so was Nora. Justice.

Nora was all smiles as she stopped. Miles saw she had blood splattered all over her face.

I have never been more attracted to someone in my entire life. When people say they have found the one. Well, I agree with them. Because I have. Kindred spirit, if that's what you call it.

"Feel better?" Miles asked.

She dropped the letter opener and rushed into Miles. They kissed hard and passionate as Miles's had imagined it to be. Paul's blood smeared onto Miles's face. Miles ran his hands up and down her back and yanked her closer to him. He never wanted it to end.

Nora pulled back. Miles couldn't take his eyes off her.

"I guess we have another place to clean up," Miles said.

"I'll help this time," Nora chuckled. "Wait. What about the alarm? He said..." Nora said.

"I wouldn't worry about that. If he told anyone, they would have been here by now," Miles said.

"I didn't think about that," Nora said. So, what do we do now? I have a handsaw in the trunk of my car," Nora said.

Miles looked down at Paul's mutilated body. Miles almost slipped on his blood as he picked him up by his shoulders and Nora grabbed his ankles. She never forgot the letter opener. It was in her back pocket. Miles knew she wanted it as a trophy. Sometimes the first one is the best one to remember. Miles had his own. His garden, so he figured Nora should have one to remember this night and what she did for Alex and her sister. They moved Paul's body slowly to the back door. Miles stopped.

Nora asked, "What is it? Did we forget something?"

"After this I have a stop to make," Miles said.

"Ok. Would you like to elaborate on that?" Nora asked.

"Later," Miles said.

CHAPTER THIRTY ONE

IT'S A BRAND-NEW DAY

SIX MONTHS LATER

Miles knew there's nothing better than the way he felt after he took a bite out of a fresh-baked beignet. Each speck of powdered sugar represented the loss and gain that had entered his life. To him, life was pretty good. As he walked down the sidewalk, he was happy, especially since he wasn't the only one anymore.

He couldn't help the smile on his face as he watched the building, which had been vacant, being moved back into. The bakery was back with bigger and better recipes. He saw one of the bakers out in the front. She was already giving samples away. The bar that was alone with Miles—well, their chalkboard grew just like their menu. They even named after him. Pike's Hike. It was a little crown with a splash of Tabasco. Hot, heavy, and will make you sweat. Miles considered it an ode to Elana.

He waved at tourists and said hi to strangers on the sidewalk and in the streets. Miles stopped in front of Petal Perfection. The shop has a fresh coat of paint, and the plants outside, which were new, thrived, always a good sign. The best sign was the one on the shop's outside. It read: "Welcome to the Re-Grand Opening of Petal Perfection."

The place was packed when he walked in.

Miles watched the man from a year ago as he stood there with his kids as they did the same thing as they searched through each flower carefully to find the perfect ones.

Miles turned his attention to the comments people had posted and reposted on social media about the shop. They said things like "perfect in every way," "stop and smell the freshness," and "Petal Perfection is perfect." Love this store and the flowers they sent my mom for her birthday.

Miles walked around to every flower station and examined the petals and stems. He tried to pick the perfect one. He heard a familiar voice. He lifted his head and saw the lady from a long time ago who wanted violets. She had changed one way, but not in others.

"I asked when the dragon fire red amaryllises will be in?" the lady asked.

She was louder than she used to be, and a little heavier. But who was Miles to judge? But it was still annoying. Miles hoped he wouldn't want to kill her this time. But he also knew wishing or imagining wasn't a bad thing. One person Miles could always count on was Davis. He was still a smartass.

"It's not their season," Davis told her.

"Well, make it happen," the woman said as she demanded.

"What do you want me to do? Pull them out of my butt and pot them for you. Sorry, not gonna happen. The thorns will seriously kill me," Davis said.

He turned halfway to show her his butt. She placed her hands up to her face, to shield her eyes.

"I never..." the lady said as she walked off.

"Well, I haven't either," Davis said as he walked after her.

Sometimes Miles wondered what went through Davis's mind.

"Hey, boss. You got a delivery," Davis said.

Davis handed Miles a large manila envelope. It was light. Miles knew what it was. Davis watched over my shoulder as Miles opened it. It was the paperwork Miles had been waiting for a while now. On top was New Orleans Freedom Bank, and the paperwork was the official return of the building and land that Heathcliff paid off.. Miles scanned the cover letter, and read that all the properties Heathcliff purchased on the street were deemed null and void and were returned to their original owners.

"Who knew what a loon he was," Davis said.

If only you knew.

"I couldn't have said it better myself," Miles said. Miles stuffed the paperwork back inside. "How is the new place working out?"

After a few months, Davis left the apartment but didn't move back with Renee. Instead, with Miles and Nora's help, they moved into a new place. A house.

***

Davis and Renee opened the front door with the biggest smiles Miles had ever seen.

"Ahhhh! Check it out!" Davis said.

"I still say we could have fit our apartment on the first floor," Renee said as she walked in a circle.

Boxes were still stacked against the walls in the living room, dining room and some are at the bottom of the stairs.

"I have to thank you again for helping us," Davis said.

"When I saw it I knew you had to have it," Miles said.

"Hell, yeah, it's a great place. And it was cheap. I still can't figure out why it was," Davis said.

"Don't look a gift horse in the mouth, Davis. Take it and be happy," Miles said,

"Hey babe. Looks like the cleaners couldn't get that spot out," Renee asked.

David, Renee, and Miles saw there were dark little red spots on the floor like paint. David bent down for a closer look. With his fingertips, he tried to rub it off.

"Looks like it's in the wood and been there a long time," Davis said. He looked over the rest of the floor. "Strange how it's just in that on area."

"I wouldn't worry too much about it. Some of these houses have their own character," Miles said.

"Character. I like that," Renee said.

"Yeah, my place all kinds of spots, streaks – the house is great. Wanna show me around," Miles said.

"Oh, you have to see where I am going to put the garden, boss," Davis said.

"I love gardens," Miles said.

Miles followed Davis and Renee down the hall, when he turned around and flashed a grin at the red spots.

Hello, Paul.

***

Miles stood next to Davis and put his arm over his shoulder and said, "I'm happy for you and Renee. You deserve it, Davis."

"You deserve it too. After everything you have been through it's nice to see you happy again. How's it going with Annabelle?" Davis asked.

Annabelle.

"Good. She's good," Miles said.

On television, a reporter popped on the screen. Davis pointed it out. Miles saw Elana's picture and Davis turned the volume up. For Miles the room went silent as he focused on what was being reported by the lead anchor, Cristina.

She hasn't changed.

"One year ago, I reported on human remains that washed up on the shore of Lake Conroe. After some time, they were found to be Elana Stansbury. The daughter of Edward Stansbury," Cristina said. "I am happy to say there has been an arrest. And it's shocking."

I haven't seen her picture in so long, I almost forgot what she looked like. AH, the memories.

Then, the Captain of the New Orleans police department stands behind a podium. Nora's dad.

"Today is a great day. We are happy to say that the streets of New Orleans are once again safe from the monster who took Elana's life," Captain Asher said.

"We have footage of Heathcliff Morand's arrest," Cristine said."

The camera shifted to footage of Heathcliff's house. Miles watched intently at the screen. The police dragged Heathcliff out of his home, still wearing his pajamas and a gray open robe, while his wife and daughters looked on. He attempted to stop on the front steps, but the officers pulled him down and towards one of their vehicles. Heathcliff noticed the cameras and directed his gaze straight into them.

"I didn't do anything. I'm innocent. I was set up," Heathcliff said.

The camera panned to the crowd and Miles saw among them, Nora. Miles started to grin, then stopped himself. He knew she had to be there just to watch.

"No. No. You can't do this to me. I help pay your salary," Heathcliff said as the doo is shut in his face.

I hate to tell you. The evidence is overwhelming. It wasn't a smart move to use her credit cards for your own selfish needs.

Mr. Stansbury came onto the screen.

"I want to thank the New Orleans police department for their hard work and for never giving up on finding my daughter's killer," Mr. Stansbury said. "She was my world.

Mant reporters chimed in and bombarded him with questions. He picked one from the leading news channel in the city.

"Mr. Stansbury, if you could say one thing to him. What would it be?" the male reporter asked.

"That's easy. I hope when they place the needle in your arm. I hope you feel it and think of me. Burn in hell. Now if you excuse me. I have a meeting to attend. Oh, I am having an open house for those who want to invest in my new gallery. For Elana. And the website will be up soon," Mr. Stansbury said.

Miles wasn't surprised Mr. Stansbury mentioned his gallery. It was more of a child to him than Elana was.

"Here at Channel Thirteen, we send out condolences to Mr. Stansbury, family and friends," Cristine said as she turned to another camera.

Good thing I called the tip line anonymously.

"You ok, boss?" Davis asked.

"Yeah, yes, I am. I'm just happy it's all over. But nothing can bring Elana back. I *loved* and *still* love her so much. She wasn't a perfect person. No one is. But she was to me," Miles said.

If I learned anything is that things happen for a reason. You may not know what it is, but you can figure it out. And if you still can't break some rules, you might just be the answer.

"In other news, the body of Farrah Reed also known as Fairy to her close family and friends has been laid to rest. We have learned she was the best friend of Elana Stansbury. An investigation is under way," Cristine said.

Rest in peace, Fairy.

Miles looked at his watch. He walked around the counter and headed toward the door.

"I gotta go," Miles said.

"Where are you going boss?" Davis asked.

Davis watched with interest as he slightly grinned. Miles ignored it.

"You got this?" Miles asked.

"You can count on me. Tell Annabelle I said hi?" Davis said.

Halfway out the door, Miles turned and leaned back inside, where he picked up a simple white rose from one of the vases. He then heard Davis, who stared at him as he leaned on the counter. Before he headed back out, Miles stopped. He just had to say something.

"We are not dating. We are just friends. Fellow shop owners who understand the highs and low of running a business," Miles said.

"Keep telling yourself that one, boss.," Davis said.

***

Miles passed a lot of people while he headed down the sidewalk. Fast with Annabelle on his mind thanks to Davis.

What could he say about Annabelle? She was one of the new shop owners, owning a shop called Hex & Tea, a few streets over. She sold the most extraordinary things, like voodoo dolls, charms, and crystals, and she read palms. She was the best. Most importantly, she was loyal. She enjoyed surprising Miles with small gestures, such as sending a text message to check in on his business. Sometimes she brought him lunch.

There are times when I find little notes inside the lunches. Nothing outrageous or over the top. They say things like, "Have a good day," "Thinking of you," and "How about a dinner meeting?" She is absolutely perfect. There's not a thing wrong with her. I wish I could say there is. But then I would be lying. She keeps me on my toes, that's for sure.

It was an accident that we ran into each other, but Annabelle says it was fate.

**

Miles's arms were full of boxes which caused him not to see where he was going. He tripped. The boxes flew everywhere on the sidewalk. He tried to gather them up before anyone could step on them. When the most amazing thing happened. Miles met her.

"Let me help with that." *A female said.*

Miles like her voice. It had this hum in it. He noticed it in those few words that it hit low and high notes in a fantastic remix. When Mile looked up, and he saw a woman dressed like a laid-back version of Wednesday Addams. Her hair glistened in the sun and shaded parts of her face at the right time. Her eyes were deep blue like an ocean explored. He liked her hands. They were slender and she had slender hands. Her cheekbones are pale with a dash of pink, and her lips were deep red, like blood.

"Thank you," Miles said as he gathered some nearby boxes.

"You're welcome" the female said.

She held out her hand and smiled. Angelic.

"Annabelle," Annabelle said.

"Miles," Miles said.

They shook hands.

***

We DO have a lot in common. But she's not you, Nora. Oh, no. I'm going to be late.

"She's gonna kill me," Miles said to himself.

CHAPTER THIRTY-TWO

WE'LL NEVER WILT

It's been a year since I've been here.

The clouds rolled in as Miles stepped onto the grayish dock. At the end of the dock, the bleached wooden planks, He had made the walk twelve times. Each one is different. But the feeling was the same, and with every step he took, Miles was reminded of his first flower.

His mom.

***

Miles watched as his mom clipped the end of a slanting bundle of flowers off. He heard her hum the same tune every day. She always told him if he wanted to keep a flower for a longer period of time, then he should cut the end in a slanted position. Add a pinch of sugar to the water but not too much or you could kill it. Just a pinch because it caused it to bloom, the sweetness began its petal life and softens, which made them soft to the touch, and the flower's aroma hung around a little longer than usual.

She set the flowers down with love and ease, as if they were a treasure. She never made an arrangement or bundle them up until each flower is in perfect position in the vase, even and perfect.

Miles opened the back door and walked further inside. She never heard him walk in.

She taught me how to do it. She made me do it. She became the person she promised she wouldn't.

She glanced up through the glass of the frame hanging on the wall in front of her. She saw me as Miles stood behind her. She stopped humming and stared at Miles. He couldn't tell if she was smiling because of the picture of her and me or because this is it.

My father was not the best person. He was a downright abusive fucker who cheated on my mother constantly and treated me like a fucking disease because he thought I was his blood. I am.

With my arm extended, Miles took aim with her favorite cast-iron skillet.

Eventually, Miles's dad left. Miles never got to experience a father-and-son bond. Honestly, he was all right with it. Miles had his mom, and She was everything to him.

And still is.

Miles never moved. He never saw her because he was staring at the exact spot he wanted to hit.

"Remember what I taught you," mom said.

She wasn't scared, nervous, or shocked; she had been waiting for this for years. She wanted this. He took one second and glanced at her.

"I love you, baby boy," mom said.

Miles thought she would have closed her eyes, but she kept them on him.

Miles reared back and swung. He hit her on the side of the head.

Her body made a thud as she hit the floor. Miles never stopped hitting her until she stopped moving. Her blood splattered on the walls and the mirror. Blood was everywhere.

After forty-six hits, Miles lowered the skillet. Her blood dripped from it to the floor, and it made a small puddle. Out of breath, Miles stared at himself in the mirror. He breathed a sigh of relief.

I step to the end of the dock, lay the white rose on the edge, and rest my palms over the stem.

She became the person she promised she would never be, just like my father. Miles learned she had had an affair with a married man. The pastor of our church. And it didn't matter to her whether he had kids or a devoted, beautiful wife. To Miles, she wasn't just selfish; she was a liar. She kept telling him that was what God wanted. He knew what needed to be done; it needed to be painful.

She created the rules, and Miles was the one who inflicted them. His mom was his first flower, not because he loved her but because he needed to practice his planting in case, he ever did it again.

***

With his eyes closed, Miles took in the peace and tranquility that surrounded him as the sun began to peak through the storm clouds. The warmth beams down, and for one brief second, everything is different in the daylight. Water splashes against the large algae-covered wooden posts that stretch deep into the lake. His lake. He rubbed the stem of a single white rose between their fingers. The thorns pierced his skin. The trees that lined the lake seemed to reach out to him. For once, they were here for themselves. There's something wonderfully haunting about this day. They wanted to thank his mom. His mom did teach Miles something. That was the rules.

Miles wanted a relationship based on honesty and respect. We wanted the best and worst of them, and he wanted to be the best version of himself. They had the best of me. If they broke one, forgiveness wasn't an option.

Miles exhaled long and hard as he saw blood on his fingers. If it could, it would drip like tears into the water. He had never felt pain like that before. It was nice. It sounded crazy, but it was true. He felt something. And liked it. Each thorn represented his love and the love he wasn't going to let go.

It was hard to admit, given the circumstances, but each one of them was selfish and broke his heart. They were the best thing that ever happened to me. He thought that he was enough. But in the end, he wasn't. He couldn't give them what they needed, asked for, or begged for.

Maybe I am damaged goods.

Miles dangled the rose over the side and pulled the petals out. The water's ripples took the petals on the surface out to find his mermaids and now sirens. Miles's floating flowers. But there was one flower that stuck out more than any of them. One he couldn't pluck.

Her petals are perfect. Delicate and thriving, it refused to leave me. He stepped back and took a deep breath. Miles thought, could all of this be over? Is it over? His head said one thing, while his heart told a different story. But he had to push it all back. Nothing was as simple as he imagined it to be.

The white picket fence, the two-story house, no "Hi, honey," or "I love you." Miles had to gamble. He won and lost twelve times. Twelve times! I know they are with me, six on either side. I imagine them standing right behind me, six on one side and the other six on the other; they always hovered, watched, and forever haunted me.

So, he gave it one last roll and landed on snake eyes.

As he gazed at the calm and bittersweet beauty, a fisherman's boat approached from a distance. On the bank, a couple walked hand in hand, while others sunbathed and splashed water at each other on the lake side. He smiled as a slender hand slid up his arm and onto his shoulder. Miles grinned.

"You're late," Miles said.

"No, I'm not. You're early. As usual," Nora said.

Miles turned around and was shocked.

I am completely in awe of Nora.

Nora was wearing something out of the ordinary. A short pure white dress that hugged her body and cups around her shoulders as two of the buttons hung open. At the hem, blue flowers gathered wildly, as if they were in a ballet dancing. And she wasn't wearing any shoes. He should have guessed The pink strip in her hair was gone. Her hair feathered around her face, framing it like one of her pictures. Her make-up is light and made her look more natural. Nora, took his breath away.

"Wow! I never thought I'd see the day when you looked..." Miles said.

"Watch it, Nora said.

"No, I like it," Miles said.

I've embarrassed her. Not an easy thing to do nowadays.

"Well, don't get used to it. I'll be back to the old me tomorrow," Nora said.

Please, don't. I like this new you. I mean I like you old you, but this Nora. This Nora is amazing.

"I thought I would dress up, being the anniversary of the day, we met," Nora said.

"You look stunning," Miles said.

He said it once, and he would say it again. He would kill for Nora. *I know most people would say we are nothing alike. That's where they are wrong.* Miles held out his hand. She noticed his bloody hand.

"What happened?" Nora asked.

"Thorns," Miles said.

Nora wrapped her soft, lush lips around his finger. He felt her tongue slide over cut. He watched as she took his finger into her mouth and gently sucked on it. She licked her lips as her eyes met him. Miles knew she liked to tease him.

What he wouldn't give to rail her against the dock for everyone to see right then and there. But that was their game.

He imagined the endless waves that carried the rowboat they were into the middle of the lake. Nora was lying in the middle; her hands gripped the edges of the rowboat as Miles kissed her neck. He slid his hand down her curvy body, under her dress, and ripped off her panties. Face to face, he watched as she closed her eyes as he entered her. With every thrust, she moaned in ecstasy. Her breath was in his ear as she said his name, Miles, repeatedly.

But that was the closet he was ever going to get to Nora. Through his imagination.

"There. Clean as a whistle," Nora said.

Yes, it is. Gather yourself. You are here for a reason.

"Shall we," Miles asked as he kept my hand out.

"We shall," Nora chuckled as she took it.

Miles had to help her inside the rowboat. Her laughter rang out as she grabbed onto him before she almost tumbled over and into the water. Once Nora was seated, Miles balanced between the dock and rowboat, then got in.

"Someone's a pro," Nora said.

"I'll have you one before you know it," Miles said.

Miles sat down, pushed off the dock, and grasped the oars. "I'm not made for the water."

Her voice bounced off the water's surface and rippled through Mile's body every time she spoke.

"You wanna make a bet?" Miles asked.

***

Weirdly, a sense of nostalgia washed over Miles. It wasn't in a creepy way, but rather a scrapbook with Nora. He realized he had never shared this part of himself with anyone before. He glanced at her and he could tell she felt it too. There was a calmness in the air. As she listened to the oars plunge in and out of the water, a smile spread across her face, the waves vibrated the bottom of the rowboat with each stroke Miles made. It wasn't as if he had never done this before, but this time felt different.

He slid the oars in and rested on them, indifferent to the way the wooden handles pressed into his arms. There was something exciting about it. A part of him had always been hidden in the darkest corners of his mind—dark, loud, and cold—but now it was warming up under the sun's light. It was because of Nora that he was awake.

"Ok. Here we go," Nora said.

Nora pushed the anchor over. It hit the water and splashed water all over her. Miles laughed.

"You should have warned me," Nora said.

"And miss your reaction? No way," Miles said.

She swung at him. He blocked her, and she leaned forward and with barely any space, she asked, "How's the newbie?"

I love the frown you make every time you bring her up.

"Annabelle?" Miles asked.

"No, the *other* girl who own a shop around the corner from you. Yes, Annabelle," Nora said.

"As far as I know she's fine," Miles said.

"Mm-hmm," Nora said.

Nora twisted her body around. The scent of her raspberry shampoo enveloped me as he laid backward, Nora started to settle half on my lap and placed her head against his chest.

"You're jealous," Miles said.

"You wish," Nora said.

"You are," Miles said with a laugh.

We have a deeper connection, Nora. One Miles would never have with anyone else in this world. No one could take it away from them. She was like me. You are me. I never thought I would meet someone exactly like me. But here you are.

Granted, I still want you, Nora. He wanted her so badly. And it didn't matter how, over the couch, against a wall, on my shop's floor, and even drenched in other people's blood. Miles thought that they had a very toxic relationship. Yes. Yes, it is. And no. Holy shit, relationships are fucking confusing.

He let the sun's warmth beam down. Nora twirled her finger on the outside of my hand. Mile opened his eyes to the trees in the background while everything smeared like a colorful canvas.

"What do you think it's like down there? For them." Nora asked.

"I thought you went down there," Miles said.

"I did. Still, what do you think?" Nora asked.

"Dark. Cold...wet," Miles said with a chuckle.

"Very funny," Nora said.

"I thought so," Miles said.

The water rushed a little as a slight breeze came through.

"I'm serious," Nora said.

"So am I," Miles said.

Nora slapped Miles's leg. It stung, so Miles rubbed it.

"Where do you think Paul is right now?" Nora asked.

Miles pointed in all directions, still with his head and back and eyes closed, He was relaxed.

"Majority of him is over there, there, and oh, over there," Miles said.

"Ok, ok, I get it. I was a little overzealous," Nora said.

Miles raised his head up.

"A little?"

***

Nora stood over Paul and continuously stabbed him. Miles was impressed but wondered if he tried to stop her, would she?

***

Nora tilted her head up, and asked, "What?"

"You decapitated him," Miles said.

"Hey, he deserved it after what he did. I owed it to my sister. And to any woman, he would have done it to in the future," Nora said.

"I agree. He should have never tried to hurt you," Miles said.

Miles kissed the top of her head before he lowered his head again. Nora was what people call a rage or focused killer. Once she set her sights on someone – like she did on Paul – she's not going to stop or be happy until the object of her obsession is dead and buried. Or in Paul's case, mutilated and sunk.

"If there's a next time it has to be nice, clean, and tight. No screwups," Miles said.

"Hey, I'm learning," Nora said as she angled her head up a little.

Through all the research Miles had done, all the professionals said once a killer like Nora took out her target, she would return to normal. Whatever normal is for a killer like her. He doesn't even think she knows what or who she is at this point. She hasn't found herself yet. No matter what, he loved her the same and when we were together, no one mattered except us.

Smiling, I said, "I know."

Back at the dock, Miles tied a double knot in the rope. As he looked around, he noticed the lakeside, which was busy when they got here, was now deserted except for them and the fisherman's boat from earlier. How long have we been here? Miles stepped onto the dock beside Nora.

She has a curious look on her face. I know she is going to bring up Annabelle again. She's threatened.

"I have a question for you," Nora asked.

I knew it. I might as well get ready to be no, yes, she's not, and we're not dating.

"Shoot," Miles said.

"Hypothetically, if weren't in a relationship," Nora said.

"You mean if we weren't in a committed, happy, sexually charged every second of the day, go to the end of the world for each other relationship drenched in blood," Miles said.

"Exactly. And I broke one of your rules. Which one do you think I would break?" Nora asked.

Interesting. Testing the waters. Smart girl. You are learning.

"Honestly, I haven't thought about it," Miles said,

"But if you did. Which one?" Nora asked.

Miles laid in the rowboat and thought about it. He knew Nora was impatient by the way she drummed her fingers on his arm.

"I would say… it would be…not being consistent," Miles said.

"What?" Nora exclaimed. "No pick something else."

Miles laughed at her demand.

"You asked me," Miles said.

"And that's what you came up with," Nora said.

"Well, you were late," Miles said.

Nora rolled her eyes, sat up, turned to Miles, and said, "I hit every red light coming here, and not to mention I couldn't pass the bazillion old grandpas that were in front of me. So, you can't pick that. I have an excuse," Nora said."

Sorry, but you asked," Miles said.

"Well, that isn't fair," Nora said.

"Prove it," Miles said.

She slipped on her mirrored sunglasses. Miles saw himself in their lenes. Nora turns back around, and said, "I don't have too."

She settled back onto Miles. He laughed. She placed his arms around her. Miles loved the way she felt inside his arms. He loved her more than anything in the world. Maybe even more than his garden of girls. He kissed her on the top of the head.

After some more time on the water, they are back at the dock. Nora leaned against the dock's railing and stared at the lake. Miles placed his hands on either side of her. He clenched his fingers around the railing tight. He pressed his body against her and stared with her.

"FYI, I would give you a second chance. Just because you're cute," Miles said.

"Cute," Nora said.

Miles nodded.

"Damn. I was hoping for something a little more inventive," Nora said as she turned and kissed his neck, "Like sexy, hot -" Nora said.

Nora's voice gradually took on the mumble of the teacher in the Charlie Brown cartoons. Miles narrowed his eyes and stared into her sunglasses. In them, he saw a figure appear from the water and began to wave at him.

"Hey. Over here," a male's voice yelled.

Miles stopped Nora and moved her from his view. In the water was a scuba diver who looked green in the face, and frantic still in the water. Alone.

"What?" Miles hollered. "I can't hear you."

"I said call the police. I found a head," the scuba diver said.

Nora jerked her sunglasses off. He didn't have to look at her to know she felt the same. Confused, lost, and now caught.

"What the fuck did he just say?" Nora asked.

"You found what?" Miles yelled.

"I found a head," the scuba diver yelled.

Miles knew something wasn't right earlier. He kept his eye on where the scuba diver was and waited. The scuba diver's boat had been sitting in the same spot for far hours, even longer than when he and Nora arrived.

"Shit," Nora said.

She paced and Miles grabbed her hand to calm her. There was no need to make a scene when there already was one. Miles had to conclude that yes, the scuba diver had found Paul. And yes, if the police showed up, and once they learned who he was, Nora was to be the one of the people they would look at. With her and Paul's ties and history, she was more than likely to be the prime suspect. Not to mention Davis and Renee lived in Paul's house.

One thing is the scuba diver didn't mention Miles's garden, which was a relief. But the scuba diver was in the area. In fact, he was only ten feet away. Miles waved the scuba diver in so they could call the police. He hoped back into his boat and was headed their way.

I can't let him take Nora from me.

"What do you have in your car?" Miles asked.

"A tire iron," Nora said.

"I hope you have some rope," Miles said.

"Never leave home without." Nora said.

Miles could feel excitement as it radiated off her like a snake examining their prey before its strike. It was infectious.

"Time for a lesson on how to make people quietly disappear in the daylight," Miles said.

Miles heard Nora run off the dock as the scuba diver made his way toward Miles. He glanced around and saw he still had a few concrete anchors. But there wasn't enough. He knew one thing they would have to send the scuba diver headfirst. Guess it's time for them to have their garden.

I have broken my rules for you because I know our love will never wilt.

THE END

THE STORY CONTINUES IN

DARK STEMS

EPILOGUE

DARK STEMS – FIREPOWER

1

Ash might as well have rained down in Annabelle's store, Hex and Tea. The police said it had burned down because she left a candle lit. Miles knew that was impossible. Annabelle never did that; she had a routine and followed it religiously. The last part of her day was to blow out all the candles. He was confident she had nothing to do with this. The police classified the fire as an accident.

Annabelle picked up a small, burnt voodoo doll among the other things. She sighed loudly. Miles felt bad for her. He had watched her work so hard. There was a chill in the night. Miles walked over, slipped off his jacket, and placed it over her shoulders. Instead of falling down the rabbit hole, it's filling up with water all around her as her world burns on all sides of her.

"I can't believe it's all gone," Annabelle said.

"No. it's not ALL gone. I bet insurance will over it, especially with the sign-off from the police and fire inspectors," Miles said.

"What's the point?" Annabella said.

She kicked the candle.

"Annabelle," Miles said.

"I don't even have a place to go. The cops said I can't stay here because of the soot and smoke damage that reached my apartment upstairs. I have no one," Annabella said.

"That's not true. You have me and Davis. And the apartment above Petal Perfection," Miles said.

She turned to Miles. Her expression was somber. Miles could see tears in her eyes, which she was trying to hold back. Miles was impressed by how strong she was.

"I couldn't," Annabella said.

"You can and will. And you can stay there as long as you want. Plus, I'll help clean your shop and get you back on your feet – hell, you can even sell your store items there. I can set up a small area in the back for you. Besides, I could use the company late at night," Miles said.

"I..." Annabella said.

Miles wasn't going to hear it and interrupted her.

"No, I don't wanna hear it. You are going to work and live with me – not live with me, but stay at my apartment for however long, it takes to get this place's grand opening ready for the second time. Again.," Miles said.

Miles knew she didn't have a choice, and she accepted it.

"Thank you, Miles. You are very kind," Annabella said

"What are friends for if you can't call on them, right," Miles said.

Annabelle's smile is so sincere, and warm. Her touch is clammy and sticky as she touches Miles's arm. He became nervous, and fast.

"What are friends for. I'll go see what I can get from upstairs. If they will let me," Annabella said.

Miles grabbed her hand and looked into the icy blue eyes – there's so much shock and pain in them. She wasn't faking or milking the loss of her shop or stuff like some people do. Miles knew she needed him. And he was going to be there.

"If they don't – don't worry. I know Renee wouldn't mind if you wear some of her things. She left a lot of upstairs from some fashion shows she was in years ago," Miles said.

Their fingers tickled each other's palm as Annabelle slid and walked away. Her curly long blonde almost whitish hair slides off her shoulders as she held onto the edges of Miles's jacket at her collarbone. There was something about her that drew Miles to her. He wasn't sure what it was, but he liked it. She was such a good person.

**

Opening the front door to the apartment, Miles flipped the light on, and it took a few minutes to pop on.

"It always does that. Don't worry, I will check it out in the morning," Miles said.

Miles put down Annabelle's small duffel bag on the coffee table. He noticed that had even been slightly scorched. He suspected that the fire wasn't an accident and that someone was trying to send a message for some reason. But who could that someone be? And who was the message for? Annabelle? Or was it for him?

"I know it's not much. It's small," Miles said.

Annabelle walked in and scanned the room, starting from the right and moving to the left. She took the two steps, which led across the cracked white tile floor and onto the blue candy-striped area rug under the dining room table, which resembled a large television tray. The plain tan walls offered little to look at, except for a black wall clock, which had dead batteries. In the room, there was also a brown leather couch concealed by a tan couch cover, a simple small TV with antennas, and a dark hallway leading to the bedroom.

"It's perfect. I promise I will be gone before you know it," Annabelle said.

Miles picked up her bag, walked past her, and head to the bedroom and said, "Nonsense. Stay as long as you want, I said that already, didn't I?"

"You did, but I'm not the type for doing something like this," Annabelle said

She leaned forward on the back of the couch. Miles glanced back one last time before disappearing into the hallway's darkness.

As Miles walked out, he said, "Seriously. It's not charity or something like that. Just – I would want someone to help me."

"And your girlfriend won't mind?" Annabella asked

"Nora? No, she won't," Miles said.

"Really"" Annabella asked.

"She's not like that. Jealous I mean. She completely trusts me," Miles said.

"Oh good. No, wait, I didn't mean it that way it came out," Annabelle said.

Miles knew she was happy to hear that.

"I know. Nora can be difficult at times and her looks – well she looks like she's cutting your head off at times. But deep down she's one of the most amazing people in the world. She's one of the most people in my life," Miles said.

She doesn't have a choice now. Even with soot marks, Annabelle is pretty. Porcelain skin, rosy cheeks – what am I doing?! What am I thinking? She's a fellow shop owner. One with a burnt down shop, here in my apartment. Sweaty. Glistening skin...I need to get the fuck out of here.

Miles and Annabella stood silent for a moment.

"Ok, there are a few towels in the closet, Renee's clothes are in boxes and drawers – even Davis as a few things. But you don't want to wear them. That would be...weird," Miles said.

"Yeah, it would," Annabelle said with a smile.

Leave dumbass

"Ok, yeah. I will see you in the morning. I'll begin beignets and iced coffee," Miles said.

He began to walk out the door. He stopped. He turned around. Annabella stared at her with her doughy eyes. Miles thought he should stay for a while. Hang out. Watch a movie or talk about anything and everything.

I can't tell if she wants me to leave, or not. I can't read her. Rarely happens to me.

"You don't mind coffee and beignets, do you?" Miles asked.

Stupid question. I know she eats and drinks – what the hell am I doing?

"Yes, and I will see you in the morning, Bright and early," Annabelle said. "Or I can meet you at my shop."

"Meet you at Hex. Goodnight, Annabelle. If you need anything I'm a text or call away," Miles said.

"Goodnight.," Annabelle said.

Miles stood as she closed the door and left him in the small hallway alone.

\#

Miles couldn't help it. He had to know what Annabella was doing. So, he walked back inside, carefully and quietly.

He opened the door to find my jacket hung over the couch. Her soot-covered long white nightgown was on the floor in a small bundle.

"Annabelle? Annabelle?" Miles asked.

There was no answer except for the start of the shower. Miles knew this was not a good idea. He stepped around the clothes scattered throughout the hallway. Miles made his way through the archway, leaned forward, and listened.

"Annabelle. I, uh. Wanted to tell you..." Miles said.

I know she can't hear me. Shit, don't do this. This is a bad idea. Just turn around, walk out, and see her in the morning. She's singing. She has a great voice.

Every step Miles took towards the steam-filling bathroom, Annabelle's voice grew louder. Miles's heart raced as he fidgeted, which was something he never did. She was so interesting. He wanted to know more about her. At the door, he placed his hands on the outside, leaned his ear close and listened. He loved the way her voice was lyrical and hypnotic. He slid it down to the doorknob. He hesitated for a moment before he bent down to look through the keyhole.

Peering through, he saw Annabelle weave through the steam as she washed her body. Miles smiled, and found it amusing how the steam obscured her figure so well which made he een more of a mystery to him.

I'm not going to do this. Get up and leave. What would Nora think? What would she say?

Just then, Miles' stomach dropped to his feet as his phone rang. He backed away and ran back down the hallway as he took it out. He knew he had to be caught. He knew it. Yet, Annabelle never came out. She continued to sing. He was relieved. Then he looked at his phone. Nora texted him.

No, no, no, no, Nora. We talked about this. You can trust me.

Miles's lips parted as he lowered my phone. He couldn't believe what he read. So, he read it one more time. It read, *"I saw your friend's place burnt down. Candles can be dangerous if you leave them lit."*

Damnit, Nora. I won't let you do this. You can't. You have to go by the rules.

His phone dinged. He had another text from Nora. It read, *"Go to the window."*

Miles walked over and pulled back the curtain. On the street was Nora. All Miles could do was stare down at her. He figured that she had been there the whole time. He watched as she placed her hands in her jacket pockets, then turned and began to walk down the deserted street.

Just then he heard the shower turn off. He rushed out of the apartment as fast and quietly as he could, carefully closing the door behind him. He leaned against it as sweat rolled down the side of face.

He walked out of Petal Perfection. Nora wasn't there. But Miles knew he had a problem. He remembered what his mom told him about a wilted flower.

"What do you do when a stem turns dark?" Miles asked.

You cut it off.

ACKNOWLEDGEMENTS

To my husband and daughter, thank you for understanding that when I am in my writing hole, typing away on weekends and late into the night, and when I ramble through a scene or chapter, whether you know what is happening, y'all always agree. I appreciate it. I love y'all more every day.

Mom and Dad, I will continue to thank you for introducing me to horror. It was the best thing ever, as we can see. Without y'all, I know I would not be here. You made sure I had opportunities that helped cultivate the writer in me. I love you so much. Plus, y'all are the best critics I could ever ask for. And when I say, to be honest, you are, In the best way, which makes me work and write harder.

I want to thank my editor, Robert Ottone for reading my wildness and making me see there is something else in the story and bringing it out in me.

ABOUT THE AUTHOR

Stacey L, Pierson has written three novels: Vale, Dark Descendants, Static, and a novella, The Breathing House through Anuci Press. Her writings have appeared in many places, most recently in *Bunker Squirrel Magazine, and RDG Books.* Her fifth, Wilt, will be published on March 27, 2025, through Anuci Press. She has been on multiple news outlets, such as KTVE Morning Show and Louisiana Living, for her writings, along with various YouTube channels. She is also a staff writer for Signal Magazine, which has published a few of her short stories.

www.ingramcontent.com/pod-product-compliance
Lightning Source LLC
LaVergne TN
LVHW010203070526
838199LV00062B/4478